COCOA in the ATTIC

for Peter
Saramarie
Rebecca
James
and Andrea

THE PACT
(24 DAYS UNTIL CHRISTMAS)

Seraphina sloshed through the crust of slushy snow collected on the sidewalk, dragging her suitcase up the absurdly steep slope toward the bright, charming building ahead with firelight flickering in its front windows and a welcoming sign that read *Spirited Inn*. She could barely feel her toes inside her soaked red Converse, and her sodden jeans clung to her calves. Although she wore the heaviest jacket she owned, the wind cut through it like she was wearing a t-shirt.

But as she came up to the building, her steps slowed, then stopped. Sera forced another step closer, then turned back and paced around a snow-covered planter.

What was I thinking? she wondered for the billionth time. *I have zero marketing experience. I've never even been a salesperson! How did I end up here? Why did I think I could possibly be a publicist of any kind? I'm going to get fired before the day's over.*

Groaning, she swept a pile of snow off the planter and plonked down, then winced. *Pretty sure my jeans just froze to the cement.*

"You know," said a voice with a hint of a laugh in it, "there are more comfortable chairs inside the inn. Next to a fire, no less. And you're not exactly dressed for the snow."

Sera looked up to see a man in his mid-twenties looking down at her with a smile. His curly black hair and heavy coat were dusted with snow, as were his black boots. Sera grimaced. The last thing she needed was some guy coming to tell her what a dork she was. "It was eighty degrees when I got on the plane. This is the heaviest coat I've got."

"Eighty? Are you serious? It's been snowing here nonstop since Halloween." He tilted his head. "You really should get inside, though. Is this your suitcase? Come on, let's go in and get you warmed up."

"I can take that," Sera protested, reaching for the handle of her suitcase as he took it. He smacked her bare hand away lightly with his gloved one.

"Keep that in your pocket. Good grief, you're going to lose a finger if you keep this up. Haven't you ever been in snow before?"

Sera made a face, following him up the stairs to the spacious porch wrapping around the inn. "I grew up in Arizona."

He groaned theatrically. "Desert girl. I'll have to keep an eye on you. Wouldn't look good if we lost bits of guests to frostbite here at the inn. I'm Kem, by the way."

"Seraphina. But everyone calls me Sera. And I'm not a guest, actually. I was hired to run the social media accounts for the inn."

"Ah, you're the famous photographer we've all heard so much about!" Kem grinned. "So why is it that you're sitting out here freezing off your talented fingers?"

Sera gritted her teeth, not eager to have that conversation with a complete stranger. Unfortunately, the stress of flying, a cross-country move, and a new job she was totally unqualified for squashed the words out of her like she had a leak in her mouth. "I'm nervous. I've never done anything like this before. I mean, I have an Instapic account, but just because I like taking pictures. I have a humanities degree, not marketing or business or anything. I'm afraid I'm going to get tossed back out on my ear."

"Not hardly." Kem opened the front door, and a welcome rush of warm air flowed over Sera's frigid skin as they stepped inside. "Felicity's been hounding the entire staff to check out your Instapage. 'Not only are her photos gorgeous, her entire account pops with warmth and joy and optimism! She's the perfect fit for our inn!' She was over the moon when you took the job."

The unexpected praise eased Sera's overworked racing heart. She managed a brief smile, then shivered violently as half-melted snow dripped off her hair and down her back. Kem's expression instantly transformed into concern. Unzipping his coat, he slipped it off and slung it around her shoulders. Sera stiffened, but before she could protest, Kem had shifted her closer to the fire blazing in the lobby and walked away, calling over his shoulder, "Warm up. I'll find Felicity so she can get you set up in your room."

Sera stood uncertainly for a second, then relented and pulled the coat closer around her. It was warm, and she was freezing.

She'd take it, for the moment.

The lobby wasn't enormous, but it was gorgeous. A grand staircase swept up the middle of the lobby, a chandelier hanging from the high ceiling. A line of wood panels paraded around the walls just above Sera's head, carved with a mural of mountains, trees, and animals. A few couches stood around the blazing fire that emanated life-giving heat. The reception desk stood to the left of the staircase, and a doorway across the lobby looked like it led into a dining room.

From the far side of the staircase, Kem reappeared with a woman at his side. Quickly tugging off the coat, Sera practically threw it at Kem with just enough of a mumbled thanks to be polite, keeping her eyes steadfastly away from him so he couldn't protest. She focused instead on the woman with him. Sera had expected the inn's manager to be a grandmotherly woman, or at least middle-aged, but Felicity didn't look any older than thirty. Her blonde curls bounced as she walked with quick steps over to the fire. She reached out and clasped Sera's hand, her bright blue eyes brimming with worry.

"Kem told me he found you wandering half-frozen in the snow," she said. "Your hands are like ice! Kem—"

"On it," Kem said, taking off again.

"I'm so sorry, Sera," Felicity said, grabbing Sera's suitcase. "Come with me. I'll show you your room so you can get dried off. The snow has been just awful this year."

"I'm sorry I got in later than expected," Sera said, following her through the lobby and into a dining room with high ceilings and intricate woodwork that changed the bright fanciness of the crystal chandeliers to a warm, welcoming glow. Her slowly-thawing fingers itched to get out her camera and start snapping pictures. The only thing that ruined the atmosphere was the persistent squeaking of her soggy sneakers. "My flight was delayed, and the roads were bad. It took a long time to get here from the airport."

"Not a problem. When I was hired on, I got stuck in an airport and arrived three days late. We're used to having to work around the weather." Felicity flashed a bright smile and pushed open the door into the kitchen. It was a stainless-steel paradise, sweet and savory smells twirling around one another in a dance that made Sera's stomach growl. Sera caught sight of Kem, now in an apron. He pressed a supersized mug into her hands as they passed, and a rich chocolate smell enveloped her. Gratitude for something hot and loaded with chocolate fought with annoyance that he'd managed to not only carry her suitcase and offer his coat, but also give her cocoa. Generally, Sera managed to freeze out any man who spoke to her before they got beyond a comment on the weather.

Still, she couldn't exactly hand the mug back over. Nor did she want to. Hot cocoa was exactly what she needed after the awful day of traveling she'd had. And Felicity was already on the other side of the kitchen. Ducking her head, Sera hurried on, escaping through another door to a narrow staircase. She and Felicity climbed to the third floor and out into an L-shaped hallway.

"The staff wing is just at the top of these back stairs," Felicity said, going down the shorter leg of the L. "Of course, you're welcome to use the main staircase if you'd prefer. But there are perks to going through the kitchen." She nodded at the mug of steaming cocoa.

"Do many of the staff live here?" Sera asked. Kem's easy grin popped into her mind, and she forced her mind irritably away from it.

"Not many. Most of the staff already live here in town, so they've got their own place. These rooms are used mostly for seasonal, temporary employees and for people who live here because they can't stand to leave work." She pointed to herself with a rueful smile.

Sera resisted the urge to ask if she was a temporary employee and asked instead, "How long have you worked here?"

"About six years. I was one of the first hired on when it opened. I love this old place, and the owner's put in a lot of TLC to make it the kind of place it is." She ran a fond hand over a picture frame, then pulled out a ring of keys. Slipping one of the keys off, she stopped at room 34 and unlocked the door. "This is yours."

The room wasn't huge, but it was plenty of space for a girl who'd spent the last four years sharing college apartments. The twin bed was made up neatly, and the furniture looked charmingly aged. Felicity opened a door across the room and said, "Here's the bathroom. Go ahead and get cleaned up, and then I'll give you the grand tour." Her phone dinged, and she checked it with a sigh. "Duty calls. I've got to go sort out a guest. Do you need anything else for now?"

"This is perfect," Sera said. "Thank you."

Felicity squeezed her arm. "I'm excited to work with you, Sera. See you in a bit."

———

Thirty minutes later, Sera was warm, dry, and savoring the last taste of the best cocoa she'd ever encountered. Begrudgingly, she admitted to herself that it might be worth staying on good terms with Kem if she got cocoa like that out of the bargain.

Pulling out her camera, she slipped the strap over her neck and headed down the back stairs. She carefully avoided Kem in the kitchen, asking another cook where to leave her mug, and slipped out into the dining room without so much as looking in his direction.

Felicity stood at the front desk in the lobby, speaking to the woman behind the desk with a wrinkle deep between her eyebrows. When Sera walked up, Felicity said, "I'm sorry, Sera. There's been a mixup with bookings and I've got to get it sorted out. Do you mind doing a little exploring on your own?"

"Not at all." Sera preferred it that way, in fact. She'd already seen a number of places she wanted to get pictures of, and on her own, she could take the time to get as many angles as she wanted. Besides, she'd been stuck in crowded airports and noisy planes all day long. She welcomed the opportunity spend time on her own.

The inn was much bigger than she'd expected from its description online. Sera had imagined an old house with maybe five or six rooms, more a bed and breakfast than anything else. Instead, there had to be at least fifty guest rooms on the second floor, several private party rooms on the third floor, and a dining room and grand parlor on the first floor.

Both the parlor and the dining room had their own fireplaces. In the parlor stood a small bookshelf filled with old, worn editions of classics—the Bronte sisters, Charles Dickens, Emily Dickinson. Sera stacked them carefully on an armchair with a colorful afghan hanging over the arm, reveling in the cozy vibes. This inn knew how to do atmosphere. Not only in its gorgeous woodwork, soft blankets, and warm smells—they even had a violinist playing a soft, sweet melody, probably piped through hidden speakers at just the right volume to influence the mood without getting obnoxious. Kneeling down, Sera pulled out her camera and went to work.

"Have you found the best room in the place yet?"

Kem's voice startled Sera right into an obstinate mood. She picked up her stack of books and returned them to their places on the shelf. "Don't you have work to do?"

Kem tossed his curly hair out of his eyes, unperturbed by her frosty tone. "I'm on break, and Felicity asked me to make sure you've seen everything. Come on, there's a room I think you'll like."

He put a hand on her back as if to guide her out. Sera flinched away, stepping out of reach. Kem pulled his hand back, but didn't stare or comment. Instead, he jerked his head. "This way."

Sera clenched her teeth. She was used to guys pressing in closer or snapping at her when she insisted on space. His total lack of reaction made her feel sheepish, and also annoyed at having been made to feel sheepish. Still, she followed at a respectable distance. That respectable distance increased a little when he headed behind the grand staircase in the lobby, where the lights didn't reach so brightly.

"Here." Kem pushed open a door directly behind the staircase and gestured inside with a flourish. Light poured out from the mysterious room, so Sera gathered her frayed nerves and slipped past him.

Just inside, she stopped, her eyes widening. It was a library—a long, narrow library that must have stretched the entire back length of the house. Shelves lined either side, a parade of comfortably worn-out spines. Classics, modern authors, kids books, nonfiction—there was a book for every interest. Armchairs, couches, rocking chairs, and bean bags filled the non-book-filled spaces. An older gentleman had fallen asleep over a book in a distant armchair. Two young kids pored over a comic book in a giant bean bag. And all Sera wanted was to pull two or three books off the shelf, sink into the nearest seat, and not move for the rest of the day.

"I thought you might like it," Kem said, hovering in the doorway. "It seemed to fit you. Quiet, cozy, and full of books."

How had he nailed her so completely within an hour of meeting her? Sera had spent so long keeping a careful barrier around her that being seen was unnerving. Without thinking, she scowled at him and backed out, heading for the safety of the lobby. Before she could get out from behind the grand staircase, a hand closed over her arm. Sera jerked away with a surprised gasp, coming away with her fists raised, only to see Kem holding up his hands defensively.

"Sera," Kem said softly, "I'm sorry if I've made you uncomfortable. I was just trying to help."

Mortified tears burned at the back of Sera's eyes. She forced them back. Travel had worn her down, rubbed the rawness of her scars, raised memories she didn't want raised. But though habit told her to keep Kem at a distance, logic pointed out that he'd done nothing to deserve it.

"I'll leave you alone if you want," Kem said, watching her uncertainly. "I've obviously done something to upset you."

"No, you haven't," Sera said, her cheeks flushing. She searched for an acceptably vague explanation, but, strained as she was, nothing came to mind before the words started spilling out. "It's just…there was a guy. Once. That I dated. And…he wasn't who I thought he was."

Sera touched her cheek automatically, just under her left eye, but she forced her hand back to her side the second she realized she'd done it. Great. Now he knew that she was not only unstable and unpleasant, but a terrible judge of character, too.

But Kem didn't shy away or make an awkward break from the conversation. Instead, he stayed very still, the way someone does when they're trying to not spook a skittish horse. "I'm sorry," he said, so much empathy in his voice that Sera felt her knotted insides relax a hair. "I'll back off if you want me to. But I promise, I'm just looking to be friendly, nothing more. I'm willing to swear a solemn vow to stick to the friendzone if that'll put your mind at ease." He gave her a sheepish smile. "And I'll be honest. There aren't a lot of people our age on the staff. I'm kind of dying for someone to talk to who isn't either a high schooler or over forty."

He hadn't berated her for being judgmental or pathetic. He hadn't even gotten all stiff and awkward the way her brothers did when she opened up. And…the thought of having a friend among the unfamiliar faces there at the inn was tempting. Especially a friend in the kitchen.

"Fair enough," Sera said, relenting. "I'm all right with a friend."

"Right," Kem said, all business now. He raised his right hand. "I, Kemuel Martin Lancaster, freely and fully vow to restrict myself to the friendzone in all our dealings." He grinned and stuck out his hand. "Good enough?"

Sera laughed, the worry that had sat heavy in her chest all day lightening. "Good enough for me," she said, shaking his hand.

"Great." Kem clapped his hands together. "You just made friends with the best pastry chef above five thousand feet. Welcome to Spirited Inn."

TWO WEEKS POST-FRIENDSHIP PACT
(10 DAYS UNTIL CHRISTMAS)

The dining room was nearly empty when Sera pranced into it at the end of the day, too delighted to pretend any sort of decorum. She scooped up an armful of dishes from an empty table on her way into the kitchen and executed a perfect Broadway-style twirl with the stack in her arms, winking at a little girl in the corner who giggled at her antics. Bouncing into the kitchen, Sera left the dishes on the counter and came to a stop next to Kem, who was piping an icing poinsettia leaf onto a small chocolate cake with the tip of his tongue sticking out of his mouth.

"Poinsettias are poisonous," Sera pointed out cheerfully.

"I'll poison you if you mess me up right now," Kem grunted. "This is for the owner of the inn."

"You mean he actually does exist? I was starting to think the mysterious owner was a faceless ghost."

Finishing the final leaf, Kem straightened and surveyed the

cake with his head tilted. "Course not. The ghost doesn't *own* the inn, she just lives here."

"Ha ha." Kem had been trying to scare her with ghost stories for days, and Sera refused to be scared. "That leaf is crooked."

Kem swiped the piping bag at her, leaving a streak of red icing on her arm. "Your nose'll be crooked if you don't stop distracting me. What's got you grinning like a ghoul?"

After licking the icing off, Sera pulled out her phone and held it out for him to see the follower count. Kem squinted at it, then widened his eyes. "Didn't you just start that account when you got here?"

"Yes!" she squealed, then clapped a hand over her mouth. The other cooks laughed, and Kem nudged her in the ribs.

"This calls for a celebration," he said, clapping his hands. "I have to help set up one of the private dining rooms, then it's time for a cocoa-tasting party. I have some new combinations for you to try."

"Deal. I'll help set up. Maybe get a few photos of your poison poinsettia cake in all its glory."

Kem carefully transferred the cake to a serving dish. "Not this one. It's a *private* private—oh no."

He froze with the cake in hand as the kitchen door opened again, letting in Felicity. She caught sight of Kem and lifted an eyebrow. "That's quite the cake, Kem," she said curiously. "For a guest?"

"For Seraphina," Kem said. Sera looked at him in surprise, and he raised his eyebrows meaningfully.

"Oh, yeah," she said. "Isn't he great at decorating with poison plants?"

Felicity laughed. "You'd have to eat a lot of leaves before a poinsettia would poison you."

"Thank you, Felicity," Kem said, his chin in the air. "You might be interested to know that the inn's social media pages are exploding with thousands of admiring fans."

Felicity perked up. "Really? That's fantastic, Sera! I've been meaning to check, but things have been crazy the past couple weeks. I can't wait until tomorrow."

"What's tomorrow?" Sera asked.

Felicity turned pink. "The owner's coming back tomorrow, so I won't be the only one running things," she said, a little too nonchalantly.

Kem exploded in a small coughing fit, burying his face in his elbow and holding the cake up and out away from him as far as he could. Once he'd recovered, he held out the cake to Sera. "Better take this somewhere safe," he said in a choked voice. Puzzled, Sera reached out for the cake. He didn't let go for a second, raising his eyebrows and mouthing, *Don't drop it.* She nodded and tugged it out of his hands.

"Off to devour my cake. All by myself," she said, edging past Felicity and up the back stairs.

"You two bring out the weird in each other," Sera heard Felicity say.

Sera laughed quietly to herself. It was true. As cringy as her first-day confession had been, she was grateful it had ended up putting them solidly and irrevocably in the friendship zone. It allowed her to be open with Kem in a way she hadn't been with anyone for ages.

It didn't take long to find which of the rooms the cake belonged in. It had been decked out in twinkle lights and ivy, with candles on the table and three miniature Christmas trees in the corner. Sera set the cake gently on a corner table and took a slow turn around the room, breathing in the Christmasness of it all.

"Did the cake make it?" Kem asked, appearing in the doorway.

"Safe and sound." Sera gestured to the corner table. "What is going on?"

Kem looked around, then stepped inside and closed the door. "The owner's not coming back tomorrow. He's on his way now." He whispered so quietly that Sera had to lean in to hear. "And he's proposing to Felicity right here."

"Proposing?" A combination of automatic recoil and irrepressible romanticism swirled up in her. "They're a thing, then?"

"Absolutely. They try to be sneaky, but Felicity blushes every time she looks at him. It's kind of adorable. And hilarious."

"Felicity deserves all the best," Sera said, her voice coming out quieter than she'd have liked.

Kem squeezed her elbow. "You okay?"

"I'm fine." Sera said it with intense determination to make it true. The door opened again, letting in Mrs. Warble, the head chef, and Mr. Johansen, the head of housekeeping. Sera straightened her shoulders and cleared her throat. "What else needs to be set up in here?"

"Just this," said Mrs. Warble. She dangled a cluster of green leaves over their heads. "You two planning to break it in?"

Sera jutted out her jaw, refusing to let this nosy old woman make things awkward. Taking Kem's hand, she bowed theatrically to kiss his fingers. Kem played right into it with a high-pitched giggle and a fluttering hand at his heart.

"Yep, it works," Sera said, pivoting on her heel and marching out.

As Kem followed her, Mrs. Warble's not-so-quiet undertone followed them down the hall. "Honestly, I don't know what to make of those two. Spend more time together than a newlywed couple, but darn me if I can catch them romancing."

Sera's head snapped up, annoyance pinching her lips together, but Kem put a hand on her arm and mimicked Mrs. Warble's gossipy lilt. "Honestly, young folk these days. If I don't entangle every single soul within ten miles, I'll eat my own chef's hat!"

Reluctantly, Sera broke back into a smile. "Nosy old bat."

"Precisely. Now, how about that hot cocoa?"

"Lovely."

"Followed by some ghost hunting."

Sera groaned. "There are no ghosts in this inn."

"Maybe. Maybe not. But I happen to know that the attic storage space runs over every single one of the private dining rooms."

A slow smile spread over Sera's face. "Kem. Are you suggesting…"

"I just want to be sure my poinsettia cake isn't really poison," Kem said airily, his eyes twinkling.

"You're a scoundrel."

"You like me because I'm a scoundrel. There aren't enough scoundrels in your life."

"And a nerd."

"Guilty as charged. Are we going ghost hunting or not?"

Sera sighed. "Fine. But just so I can turn you over to the police if those poinsettia leaves turn out to be fatal."

Langdon Hyatt had not been this nervous since the day he decided to sink his entire life's savings into renovating a dilapidated old inn. The fourth time he'd called Mrs. Warble, she had threatened to boil his head and serve it in a stew if he interrupted her during the dinner rush again. So he'd settled for pacing his living room, repeatedly pulling a small velvet box from his pocket and putting it back again. It had been two weeks since he left town and he had a mountain of mail and paperwork teetering on his home desk, but he couldn't focus long enough to read any of it.

Finally, he gave up any pretense of patience and walked the two blocks to the inn, pausing just outside to survey it through the falling snow. He'd been gone before Thanksgiving was over and had missed the transformation to Christmas. Colorful lights lined the roof and circled the windows, reflecting off the snow piled on every little outcropping. The picture windows facing the street framed two seven-foot Christmas trees, decorated with tiny lights and tinsel.

Langdon shook his head, remembering the run-down building he'd sweated over and bled on through months of renovations. He'd known he needed it, even if he couldn't see then what the inn would become. That old building had brought him more satisfaction and success than he could have dreamed.

More than that, it had brought him Felicity.

A warm glow radiated out from his stomach, a rush of adrenaline churning all his limbs into motion again. He hopped up the porch stairs two at a time and crossed the porch in three long strides. Pausing briefly to finger-comb his hair back into place, he tugged the front door open and walked inside.

The late dinner guests were still in the dining room. So was Felicity. Langdon hovered in the lobby near the door, watching her go from table to table, chatting with guests with an easy grace Langdon had never been able to achieve. He might run the inn from a business standpoint, but Felicity was without a doubt the face of the inn. Without her innate ability to connect with people, to see what they needed and find simple ways to bring them joy, the inn might never have made it off the ground. He'd missed seeing the way she lit up a room just by being in it.

Felicity turned away from the guests she had been chatting with. Her eyes swept past him, then doubled back. Her inn-smile—sincere, but distinctive—softened into a smile that spread through her eyes and never failed to make Langdon catch his breath. She weaved through the tables, knocking into a chair in her haste, and slipped her hands into his.

"You sneak! You lied about what day you were coming back,"

she said, her sparkling eyes ruining her reproachful tone.

Langdon rubbed his thumb over the back of her hand. "Maybe. I like to keep you on your toes. Is this all the greeting I get?"

"We're not scandalizing the guests, no matter how long you've abandoned me here alone."

Langdon raised his eyebrow, looking around. "You weren't exactly alone."

"You know what I mean." She tucked her chin down. "I've missed you."

"I've missed you, too, Liss. I'm never spending two weeks away again, or you might just realize that you can run this place better without me. I thought you were crazy, bringing on someone just to run the social media accounts, but from what you've told me it's been another brilliant move on your part."

Felicity laughed. "It's not brilliance on my part, trust me. The girl has a gift for understanding exactly what makes this inn special and then showcasing it for the rest of the world to see. Have you seen her photos? I feel like she's gotten right at the heart of your inn."

"*Our* inn," Langdon said, pulling her closer. Felicity resisted, shaking her head.

"Not in front of the guests."

Langdon groaned. "Haven't the past two weeks been torture enough? If you won't kiss me, will you at least come to dinner with me?"

Glancing around, Felicity said, "Just let me make sure cleanup is taken care of and get my coat."

"Cleanup is taken care of. And you don't need a coat."

Felicity tilted her head, narrowing her eyes. "Did you have something to do with the fact that our chefs have been kicking me out of the kitchen all night?"

"Well, I couldn't very well have you filling up on chocolate croissants and spoiling my surprise, could I?"

Taking her hand, he led her up the grand staircase, knowing full well that Felicity almost never used it. She enjoyed escaping up the back staircase, she'd often said, and had even admitted to pretending she was the housekeeper of a grand house in days long past. But tonight, he was determined to show her that she was the lady of the house.

They passed a number of guests on the second floor, but the third floor was quiet. The second they were out of sight, Langdon spun Felicity in close and kissed her soundly, weaving his fingers into her hair and breathing in her sweet coconut scent.

"I missed you," he whispered, resting his cheek on the top of her head as she nestled into his shoulder. She sighed, a happy sigh that always melted him.

"I missed you too, Langdon. It's a wonderful surprise to have you home a day early."

Langdon straightened, putting one arm around Felicity's shoulders and slipping his other hand into his pocket to check on the small velvet box. "We haven't even reached the surprise yet. Come along, Lady Felicity. Dinner awaits."

Flushed with success and full up to her ears with warm, creamy cocoa from the inn's master pastry chef, Sera was in the mood for any adventure, even a phony ghost hunt. She followed Kem up the stairs and into a private dining room two doors down from the one where she'd delivered the cake.

"Getting up there is the tricky part," Kem said, taking the tablecloth he'd pulled from the kitchen and placing it, folded twice, on the table. Next, he placed a chair carefully on top of the tablecloth and scooted the other chair close enough to serve as a stepstool.

"Just how often do you go around spying on private parties?" Sera asked.

Kem grinned. "I've never had the guts to do it before, but I've been planning it out since I started working here. You're witnessing a dream come true tonight."

"You know," Sera said, holding the chair on the table steady as Kem climbed onto it, "when I agreed to be your friend, I didn't realize that included aiding and abetting criminal activities."

"Friendship bonus!" Kem reached over his head and spread his fingers wide over a nearly invisible panel. As he pressed upward, the panel popped out of place, and he deposited it to the side. Hoisting himself up, he disappeared into the attic space and then reached back down. "It's solid. Looks like it's even been finished up here, carpets and all."

Fighting against a wobbly feeling in her legs, Sera stepped up on the first chair, then on the table, then the stacked chair. There, she froze.

"This might be a good time to mention that I don't do well with heights," she whispered, clutching the back of the chair she stood on.

"Really? Huh. Um. Well. Don't think of it as going up through the ceiling. Think of it as coming up through the floor."

Oddly enough, that worked to loosen Sera's fingers. She reached up and grabbed the edge, and Kem helped pull her up. Once she was safely landed, Kem slid the panel mostly back into place, leaving them in near darkness.

A sudden bright light made Sera wince and shield her eyes. Kem held a flashlight under his chin, making his best spook face. "I told you this was a ghost hunt," he stage-whispered, bugging his eyes.

Rolling her eyes, Sera swiped the flashlight and shone it around the attic space. Kem was right—it had been finished at some point, though it didn't look like anyone had been here in years. She stifled a cough from the all the dust, walking over to lone box lying in a shadowy corner.

"Wouldn't you think they'd use this for storage space?" Sera asked, peering at the box. It wasn't sealed shut, so she nudged a flap open.

"Maybe it's too much of a pain to get things up and down from here," Kem said, joining her. "What's in there?"

"Letters." Sera hesitated, but the dust on the box was so thick—whoever had written them was probably dead. It wasn't prying if the letter-writer wasn't alive, right? Carefully, she pulled out the closest letter and examined the envelope. There was nothing written on the outside. It had never been mailed. Flicking through the other letters, Sera could see that none of them were addressed or stamped either, though the envelopes were obviously worn.

"Weird," she whispered, lifting the flap and pulling out the paper inside.

Mom, it began.

Kem snorted. "Here I thought we'd discovered a stash of long-lost love letters," he whispered. "It's just letters home."

"Why wouldn't they have been mailed?" Sera wondered, glancing at the full box. "Why would someone write home for years and never send them?"

"Maybe their parents died, and this was their way of coping," Kem suggested. He grinned. "I told you this was a ghost hunt. Looks like we found some after all. Maybe we'll even get lucky and hear the violinist."

Sera's skin prickled. "What violinist?"

"The inn's ghost. Haven't you been listening to any of the stories I told you?"

"Not willingly." Sera set the letter back in the box, Kem's ghost story finally getting her attention. "You never said anything about a violin."

Kem's eyes sparkled. "Ghosts don't seem so farfetched in a creepy old attic, huh?"

Sighing to cover the unwelcome twitch in her stomach, Sera said, "We're on a ghost hunt, after all. You might as well tell me the story."

"About time you softened your hard heart." Kem cleared his throat and stretched his fingers dramatically. "The previous owners of the inn had a daughter who loved to play the violin. When she was about ten, she fell out of that old oak tree behind the inn and broke her neck. Her parents tried to keep up the inn after she died, but the old-timers around here say they couldn't stick it out because they'd hear their little girl playing her violin every time they went near her room."

That first day, Sera had heard the faint sounds of a violin as she explored the inn. Was it possible…

She shook herself mentally. *No. Ghosts don't play the violin. The inn just pipes the music for the atmosphere.*

"Stories grow plenty big in small towns," Sera said dismissively.

Kem shrugged. "Maybe. But Margie—the one that owns the quilt shop down the way—she told me that when the new owner bought the place, he asked her whether there were any kids in town who played the violin."

"Coincidence," Sera scoffed. Still, she couldn't force the hairs on the back of her neck to lie down. When a door creaked open beneath them, she jumped so badly that Kem stuffed a fist in his mouth to keep from bursting out laughing and giving them away.

Felicity's voice floated up into the attic, recognizable but indistinct. Kem rubbed his hands together. "Showtime," he whispered, heading for the panel over the reserved room.

A rush of reluctance swept over Sera, and she grabbed Kem's sleeve. "Maybe we shouldn't do this," she whispered. "What if we get caught?"

"We won't get caught," Kem wheedled. "Come on, we've come this far. Might as well be complete reprobates."

Still, Sera's gut twisted nervously. Maybe it was just the ghost story getting to her, but something felt off. Something was going to go wrong. What if she got fired just when things were getting good? What if she got kicked out and had to find a lame desk job somewhere she wouldn't see Kem every day?

Whoa, girl, Sera thought, reeling in her thoughts before they got out of hand. *Those are not the kind of thoughts you need to have about someone you made a solemn friendship pact with.*

Kem took her silence as agreement and crept closer to the square panel several yards down from the one they'd come through. He motioned to Sera, and she switched off the flashlight.

"You've got the entire staff conspiring against me, even the one you haven't met," Felicity said, her voice coming in clearer as Kem cautiously worked his fingers into the crack around the panel. "Sera passed that cake off as her victory prize and swore she was taking it up to her room to devour in one sitting."

A deep laugh sounded. "I may have threatened a life here and there if anyone let my secret slip."

Kem got the panel loose and lifted it half an inch. He jerked his head for Sera to join him in peering through, but she stayed in place, still hesitant, satisfied just to listen.

"Felicity," the voice said, a tremor going through its low tones. "I can't—I never want to go through the last two weeks again. Being away from you—it made me realize how much I depend on you, how much a part of me you are."

Felicity's voice softened. "I know. I missed you too, Langdon."

Langdon. With that one name, the evening went from a harmless adventure to the emotional equivalent of sticking a finger in an electrical socket. Sera's heart rattled in her chest, her blood racing through her veins like a roller coaster car about to go off the rails. A rushing noise filled her ears, so loud that she couldn't hear what was going on below anymore. Dropping to her knees, she crawled over next to Kem, her watery elbows barely supporting her. Leaning down, she peered through the crack, holding a sob at the back of her throat as she located the man below.

It can't be. There's more than one Langdon in the world. There's no way...

She caught sight of him, and a jagged gasp escaped her. Flecks of gray mixed into his brown hair. His shoulders were broader. But his face—Sera couldn't not recognize that face.

Scrambling backward, Sera made for the vague line of light down the way, blinded by the darkness and the tidal wave of tears. With hands shaking violently, she pried the panel up, dropped it, pried it up again and shoved it out of the way.

"Sera!" Kem whisper-called after her, running as fast as he dared across the carpeted floor. "Sera, wait!"

But she couldn't wait. Swinging her legs over the edge, she dropped down. Her shaking hands couldn't hold her. She dropped onto the chair before she was ready, hit it wrong, knocked it off the table with a mighty crash and landed hard next to it. Her shoulder throbbed from hitting the table on the way down, but Sera barely noticed. The noise—he'd surely have heard the noise.

She had to get out. Stumbling to her feet, she bolted for the door. Her room. She had to get to her room.

Somehow, she made it down the hall and around the corner, skirting around a girl in a blue dress and ducking inside her room. She closed the door behind her and pressed her back against it. Squeezing her eyes closed, she curled her legs up to her chest, hugging them tight against her and pressing her face into her knees.

How could this have happened? Hadn't anyone mentioned the name of the owner before? She racked her brains, but she couldn't come up with a single mention of him as anything other than "the owner."

A soft knock made her jump, but it was only Kem's voice that came through the door. "Sera? Sera, answer me. Are you hurt?"

Sera opened her mouth, but choked before she could make a sound. She pressed the back of her head against the door instead.

"I saw you fall. I'm not leaving until I know you're alive. I'll break down this door if I have to."

The last thing Sera wanted right now was to face Kem. One look from his big hazel eyes and she would tell him everything. She wasn't ready for it all to come out, not yet. "I'm fine," she said, her quivering voice barely loud enough to carry.

"Sera, talk to me. What happened?"

Sera just shook her head, knowing he couldn't see her but too tangled up inside to speak.

"Please, Sera." There was a desperation in his voice that she'd never heard there before. "I don't understand. What's going on?"

"Go home, Kem," Sera said, her voice coming out in uneven shards. "I can't. Not tonight."

A long silence met her words, so long that Sera thought Kem had left. But then his voice came through once more. "I've got my phone on me. If you need anything, I'll come right back here, okay? Just…just keep me updated, okay?"

MORNING LIGHT
(9 DAYS UNTIL CHRISTMAS)

At some point, Sera fell asleep there on the floor. She dreamed that she was nine years old again, holding a camera while Spirited Inn collapsed around her and Felicity demanded she put it back together. Langdon was there too, not as she'd seen him the night before but gray-haired and bent with age. He simply walked away, leaving Sera in the wreckage of his inn.

A tuney bleep snapped Sera out of the dream. She pushed herself into a sitting position, rubbing the rough bumps the carpet left imprinted on her face. Her phone lay beside her with seven unread texts. She scrolled through six from Kem, her tired, anxious heart warming at his concern. Then she read Felicity's.

Could you stop by my office first thing this morning?

Oh, no. Was she about to be cut loose? And even if she wasn't—if, by some narrow chance, Langdon hadn't seen her fleeing and discovered who she was—would she really be able to stay? Knowing he was here, that she might run into him at any moment?

Sera's head dropped into her hands. Who was she kidding? Knowing that he was here, there was no way she could possibly leave. But what if he insisted she did?

There was no way to know until she met with Felicity. Dragging herself to her feet, Sera changed her clothes, pulled her hair into a messy bun, and determined that yesterday's makeup would have to do. She didn't have the energy or willpower to do much about her appearance.

Picking up her camera, Sera slung it over her shoulder automatically. She took a second to text Kem. *Meeting with Felicity. See you later today.*

She reached for the doorknob and hesitated. Pulled in another deep breath. Turned the knob and headed out.

The narrow back stairs that had become homey and comfortable felt off-kilter and strange, like walking through a Picasso painting. Maybe it was the lack of sleep. Maybe it was the fact that Sera's entire world had just tilted. Reaching the bottom, she kept her head down and hurried through the kitchen. She knew Kem would be busy with his morning duties, but she couldn't run the risk of making eye contact with him.

Felicity's office was in the back of the lobby, next to the library. Sera straightened her shirt halfheartedly and knocked.

"Come on in," Felicity called.

Sera entered. Felicity had pushed her chair into a corner and stood behind her desk, leaning against the window ledge. The sun reflected off the snow and caught the diamond on her finger with a merry twinkle.

"Congratulations." The word got stuck in Sera's throat and came out barely above a whisper.

Felicity beamed. "Thank you." Then she leaned forward, her eyebrows drawing together. "Are you feeling all right?"

Sera didn't trust herself to speak. She nodded.

"Okay." Felicity clearly didn't believe her, but she at least had the grace to move on and not press. "I have some good news for you, Sera. The work you've done with our social media accounts has been phenomenal. I did some talking with the owner this morning—" she twisted the ring on her finger— "and we would like to turn your job into a full time, permanent position. How would you like to be Spirited Inn's chief marketing coordinator?"

What? This was not what Sera had expected. Felicity had discussed it with Langdon? Did that mean—had he told her who she was?

"It's a very attractive promotion," Felicity continued on. "Salary, benefits, the lot. It will require more time from you, and you'll have to stick around during the inn's busy times. Including Christmas and New Year's."

That cut through the bewilderment binding Sera's tongue. "I can't stay through Christmas," she said automatically. "I took this job with that specific condition."

As if Sera hadn't been through enough shocks in the past twelve hours, the chair in the corner she'd assumed empty spun around. And there was Langdon, his eyebrows lowered and his tone sharp.

"Are you crazy?" he demanded. "Do you know what a huge offer that is for someone fresh out of college without even so much as a business degree? Are you really going to throw that out the window because you want to go home for Christmas?"

"Langdon," Felicity said, exasperation in her low voice. "Stop attacking her. You agreed to let me handle this."

"I'm not attacking her," he protested, leaning back in the chair. "I just want to know why it's a deal breaker."

Sera stared, dumbfounded. He looked back, waiting patiently for her response, without a hint of discomfort. The truth hit her harder than the floor had the night before: he didn't recognize her. Hurt and fury burned through her.

"Because of you," she said. The words flew out sharp and hot, ripping free from the piece of her heart that had never quite healed in over a decade. Both Langdon and Felicity shifted, eyes widening. Sera went on. "Because if Mom had another unopened stocking on Christmas morning, it'd break her all over again. Because the last time someone missed Christmas, he never came home again. And I won't do that to my family."

The blood drained from Langdon's face so quickly that spots danced in front of his eyes. Automatically, he turned to Felicity, searching for some sense and stability in what had just happened. "I thought you said her name was Sarah," he said, then clapped a hand over his eyes. Of course. Not Sarah. Sera. "You stopped going by Phina."

"When I was twelve. You might've noticed if you'd come around once in a while. Or even called. Or friggin' *texted,* Lang. Mom's been praying for you morning and night for twelve years now, you know? And you couldn't even take the time to send her an email."

The words flew at him, piercing him, shredding him. Langdon dropped his hand, staring numbly at the little sister he hadn't seen for over a decade. Little Seraphina wasn't nine anymore. Somehow, she had grown up, graduated, and landed in his inn. She was angry. And he couldn't blame her.

"Phina, I—" Langdon stumbled over the automatic nickname. "I mean Sera. Seraphina. I don't…"

"I should go," Phina said. No, Sera. *Come on, Langdon, don't lose your head.*

But it was too late. He couldn't even drag himself together enough to speak as she half-leaped, half-ran from the office.

"Langdon." Felicity's voice cut into him like a scalpel—thin, neat, and deep. "What just happened?"

The last thing Langdon wanted to do in that moment was face Felicity—the woman he loved with every ounce of his heart, the woman he'd more or less lied to through six years of employment, friendship, and eventually courtship. But she deserved an explanation. Lifting his eyes, he found her face, pale and shaky. His heart shattered. He'd disappointed her. The same way he'd disappointed his family. The way he disappointed everyone eventually. He should have known it was too good to last. He'd been living off stolen happiness with Felicity.

"I was under the impression that your family had passed on," she said. Her voice was impressively calm, but Langdon could see the pain in her eyes.

"I told you I didn't have a family," Langdon said. The words inflamed the still-raw pain in his heart. Precisely the reason he never spoke about it. "When I met you, I hadn't spoken to them for six years."

"Why not?"

Langdon blew out a breath. Why not? It was a question he'd asked himself hundreds of times, one that he could sometimes answer. Just now, with his brain and his heart in a wild jumble, he wasn't sure he could answer anything. But this was Felicity. For Felicity, he had to try.

"My dad and I had a rocky relationship," Langdon said woodenly, trying to bury himself in a rational explanation. "He didn't understand why I struggled with school, how all my siblings could be getting A's and B's while I mostly hung out down around the C's. I was supposed to be the one setting the example for the younger kids, but I was a disappointment there."

"Langdon," Felicity said tremulously. But now that the words had started, they wouldn't stop, rolling out of Langdon like a mudslide.

"I made it into college somehow. I was determined to do it right. I chose a computer science degree because that was what would make Dad most happy. I wasn't going to be the weak link. I'd make him proud.

"Except that I was still me, and I was not cut out for school.

The tests killed me. I'd go in there knowing everything we'd talked about in class. But once they handed me the test, it all vanished. I'd sit there and sweat, feeling like the paper was going to cut me into ribbons." Even now, the thought of sitting in the testing center made Langdon's stomach churn. He swallowed the ghost of his test nerves and went on. "One of my professors called me in and told me I was failing her class. It hit me hard. I'd never been great, but I'd never gotten below a C. My great plan to impress my dad was blowing up in my face.

"That night, a bunch of guys from my dorm were going drinking." The memory constricted his ribs, and he had to close his eyes for a couple of breaths. "You have to understand—my parents never drank alcohol, and we were raised with the strictest vows to keep away from it. My uncle was an alcoholic. Between seeing him drink himself into the hospital and my parents coming up with all kinds of creative threats if we ever touched so much as a beer, I'd never even been tempted to try it. But that night, I was a wreck. I knew I'd let my parents down again, wasted their money and mine on classes I couldn't pass. I wanted to disappoint them all the way, I guess. I decided to go along with my friends."

Langdon's chest ached in all the same places it had that night twelve years earlier. Every scab he'd formed was being peeled off, opening wounds he'd long since learned to ignore. He sought Felicity's eyes, desperate to connect to her.

"Once we were there...I ordered a Sprite. I just couldn't do it. I didn't want to get drunk. I didn't want to let my family down any more than I already had. But someone from my hometown saw me there at the bar with a drink in my hand. As far as I can tell, she called home and told her parents, who went and told mine." Gritting his teeth, Langdon forced himself on. "Dad called the next day. I had no idea what was coming. I was still trying to decide whether to confess that I was failing a class when I picked up."

He fell silent, struggling to find the words for what had happened next. How could it still stab so deeply after so many years? Felicity waited, silent and unreadable.

Finally, Langdon said, "Dad started yelling the second I picked up. All things that were true and hurt the worse for it. I forgot all the calm, rational things I'd planned to say and yelled back. And when I was too angry to string words together anymore, I hung up on him. And then…"

Langdon leaned his elbows on his knees, letting his head dangle. Felicity's hand rested on the back of his neck, a gentle, supportive gesture that only made Langdon cringe with another shovelful of guilt. He said, "I'd tried so hard to become what Dad wanted me to become. But after that, I gave up. I decided there was no hope for me. I was tired of trying, and I didn't want him to be able to tell me what a disappointment I was anymore. So I walked down the street to the MobileTalk store and got a new phone number. I changed my email address. And I walked out on my classes. Quit school and got a job with a construction company in a different city."

Langdon knew he didn't deserve any comfort from Felicity, but he reached back anyway to take her hand and squeeze it in his. She didn't pull away, but she didn't squeeze back, either. Sighing, he said, "I didn't think of it as cutting myself off. I was planning to go home for Christmas in a month, and if it wasn't awful, I'd give them my new number, try it all again. But when December rolled around...hard as the work was, I was happier working construction than I'd ever been in school. And I thought that if I tried to tell my dad that, he'd lose it all over again, and it would ruin the first place I'd really felt like myself."

At that, Felicity brought her other hand up to lay over the top of his. He looked up at her, expecting to find repulsion or disgust. Instead, he saw the shining streak of a tear down her cheek. Sad for him, or saddened by him? Langdon didn't dare ask.

"I didn't go home for Christmas." The words echoed hollowly in Langdon's chest. "I told myself I'd call and apologize, come up with some excuse, but nothing I thought of ever seemed to be enough. Christmas came and went. I told myself I'd call on New Year's Eve. After New Year's. In February. In the spring. The longer it went, the harder it was to think of making the call. The next Christmas was the last time I thought seriously about calling them, but I was such a coward, Felicity. I couldn't do it." Tears burned in his eyes. "Once it had gone, I decided they were better off without me."

"Oh, Langdon," Felicity whispered. "How could you think that?"

Langdon shook his head. "It wasn't hard. I couldn't do anything the way my family expected. I was a failure at setting the example for the younger kids. I was happy just being a construction worker, but—"

"*Just* a construction worker?" Felicity interrupted. "Langdon, you learned to build beautiful things. You renovated this place almost entirely by yourself. You've grown it into a thriving business, a place people love, a place people can recharge and enjoy being with each other. There is nothing *just* about you." She hesitated, then added, "If your family can't see that, it's their own fault. But I think they deserve the chance to try."

"One of them has." Seraphina's furious expression cut through Langdon's memory. "I don't think she was impressed."

"I think her reaction had more to do with the season. Christmas is obviously a difficult time of year in your family. Between the shock of seeing you for the first time in so many years and the suggestion that she not go home for Christmas...don't let it scare you off, sweetheart. Give her a chance to see you. The real you, not the version of you trying to grow up to be your father."

Langdon hunched his shoulders. Felicity gently pushed him to sit upright, then lifted his chin and looked straight into his eyes. "It's time to stop hiding, Langdon."

"I don't know if I can," he whispered.

"I do. You are stronger than you have ever given yourself credit for. Now is the time to let it show."

A gentle knock sounded on Felicity's door. Langdon swiped a hand over his eyes and cleared his throat. Felicity put a hand on his shoulder and called, "Come in."

For a terrifying second, Langdon thought Seraphina had returned. He wasn't ready to face her again, not yet. But instead, the receptionist peeked in.

"Sorry to interrupt," he said, "but I've got someone from Paints and Co here asking to talk to you about the tree trimming festival tomorrow, Miss Renner."

Langdon felt weariness spreading down his neck as Felicity nodded and said, "Thanks, Roger. I'll be out in a minute."

The door closed, and Langdon sighed. "Duty calls."

"Langdon," Felicity said, taking his hand. "What are you going to do about Sera?"

He paused silently for a long moment. From an employer standpoint, it made sense to do all he could to keep Sera there. From the standpoint of their complicated history... "I'll let you know when I figure it out."

<hr />

Sera was half-blind with fury when she barreled out of Felicity's office. She smacked straight into Kem, who opened his mouth to say something. Before he could get the words out, Sera took off again. Up the main staircase to the third floor, down the hall to the private dining room she and Kem had invaded the night before. It sat in perfect form, no hint of the turmoil that had taken place there only hours ago. Sera stacked the chair up on the table, popped the attic panel out of place, and climbed up.

The box of letters sat right where she'd left it, one flap standing up in a jaunty wave. She sat beside it, stared at it, reached in and pulled out the envelope lying on top of all the others.

Without a flashlight, the attic was much too dark to make out the words of the letter, but Sera remembered the twist in her gut as she'd read the greeting the night before. *Why would someone never mail their letters home?*

Unfolding the paper inside, Sera scooted back over to the open square leading down to the dining room. By the light coming in, she could just barely make out the signature on the bottom.

Langdon.

But knowing that he had written those letters only opened up more questions. *Why* wouldn't *he have mailed them home? There must be years' worth of letters in there. Why write to a family he didn't care about? If he did care, why didn't he at least try to talk to us? Why not send the letters? He can't have forgotten our address. Why wouldn't he have just picked up the phone and called?*

A noise made her shift her gaze wearily to the room below. Kem climbed up on the table, up on the chair, up into the attic. Sera sat there with the letter in her hand, staring at it dully, too full of bewilderment to speak.

"I heard what you said to Mr. Hyatt," Kem said softly.

Sera looked at him, then looked away, not sure whether to be upset or relieved.

"I wasn't trying to eavesdrop," he added quickly. "I just wanted to be sure to catch you before you left Felicity's office. You scared me last night. But now…that must have been awful, to have that sprung on you."

Sera nodded mutely.

"What did Felicity say?"

Sera blew out a breath. "She offered me a full-time position. But she said I'd have to stay over Christmas, I told her I couldn't, then Langdon popped out of the corner and basically told me I was an idiot to pass up the position just for Christmas." She clenched her fists, squeezing her eyes shut. "He didn't even recognize me, Kem. We were face to face, and he had no idea who I was. I got so mad, not because of what he said, but because he can still hurt me. He's been gone for twelve years. Why should I care anything about him?"

Kem scooted over and put an arm around her. His warmth seeped into her tense shoulders. Sera's gut reaction was to put space between them, but it felt good to have him so close. She didn't have the strength to push him away. And after all, they were just friends. It was okay to lean into him, to take comfort in his nearness.

"I think you care about him because you have one of the biggest hearts I've ever known," Kem said softly. "Family doesn't just stop being family. And if these letters are what I think they are," he added, gesturing to the paper in her hands, "I think Mr. Hyatt might need rescuing. And I can't think of a better person to do it."

Rescuing? The peace of the moment evaporated in a swift flare of temper. Sera tossed the letter on the ground and stood, a wave of cold stinging her shoulders as Kem's arm fell away. "He abandoned us, not the other way around," she snapped. "Why should I drag him back to a family he doesn't want to be a part of anymore?"

"Sera, wait," Kem called, but Sera was already dropping down into the dining room. She jumped from the chair, hitting the floor with a jolt. She stopped briefly at her room to grab her coat,

boots, and gloves—she'd learned her lesson after that first day—
and then went downstairs.

Thankfully, Langdon was nowhere in sight. But Felicity stood
at the reception desk with a balding man in a garish orange tie.
Ducking her head, Sera made for the door. She heard Felicity say,
"Excuse me for just a minute, please." Sera walked faster, but
Felicity caught her just before she made it to the front door.

"I know you must need some time," Felicity said, her voice
low and her eyes full of empathy. "Take what you need. But
Sera…please give him a chance."

Over Felicity's shoulder, Sera caught sight of Langdon coming
out of Felicity's office. He stopped by the grand staircase and met
Sera's gaze, his eyes red and his face haggard. With difficulty, Sera
pulled her attention back to Felicity.

"I need to walk," Sera said, fumbling behind her for the
doorknob. "I'll be back later."

The doorknob turned, and Sera escaped into the frigid morning.

Sera had spent enough time the past two weeks exploring the
tiny town of Starling to know all the best places to duck in long
enough to thaw out. Even so, by the time she returned to Spirited
Inn, her coat was stiff with snow and ice, her fingers were cold
inside her gloves, and her toes were numb inside her snow-
crusted boots. The bright stars shone down through the crisp,
cold air, and the flickering firelight visible through the windows
of the inn was a welcome sight.

She pushed the front door open. The receptionist caught her eye and looked down at his phone. A second later, Kem came out of the dining room, his forehead creased with worry. He helped her tug her gloves off and pushed a blessedly warm thermos into her frozen hands. He took her coat and went to hang it up in the coatroom, then plucked a blanket off one of the couches in the lounge and wrapped it around her shoulders.

"I've got dinner in the kitchen for you," he said. "Come on, I'll warm it up."

A few workers were still in the kitchen, cleaning up the dinner mess. Sera, not in the mood for friendly kitchen chatter, went through to the back stairs and waited there, sipping the cocoa from the thermos, until Kem appeared with a steaming bowl of broccoli cheddar soup and a crusty roll.

"Come on," he said, jerking his head at the stairs. "Let's go up and find somewhere quiet to eat."

He led the way to one of the private dining rooms. Sera didn't want to sit at the table. She'd spent too much time climbing up on one the past couple of days. Instead, she put her soup and cocoa on a chair and sat on the plush carpet beside it, pulling the blanket up over her head like a hood for added warmth. Kem sat beside her, letting her eat in silence until she was about halfway through her bowl.

"Can I tell you something about me?" Kem asked hesitantly.

Sera looked up from her soup, surprised. "Of course."

Kem folded his legs up to his chest and wrapped his arms around them, resting his chin on his knees. But he didn't speak.

Sera looked at him—really looked at him for the first time since she'd walked into the inn that night. Maybe for the first time ever. She'd always been half-afraid to see him too deeply, afraid she would make the same mistake she'd made in college. It was safer for them to be friends, safer to not let it go beyond anything fun and lighthearted and superficial.

But this wasn't the same joking, laughing Kem she'd seen so often. His hazel eyes were far away and tinged with pain, and a worried wrinkle sat just between his eyebrows, nearly concealed by the black curls that fell over his forehead. Impulsively, Sera reached out to grip his forearm. Kem looked up, startled. Sera held out the thermos. A tiny smile appeared, and Sera realized that he had dimples. How had she missed that before?

Kem took a drink from the thermos, then sighed and spoke with his eyes fixed on the carpet. "When I was three years old, my mother left me with her parents and took off. I didn't see her again for years. She called once in a while, but usually didn't want to speak with me. I grew up so angry. Angry that she had left me, that she didn't care enough to even talk to me. Angry at my grandparents for letting her get away with it."

A lump grew in Sera's throat. She could hardly imagine the Kem she knew as an angry child, but she could see the pain in his eyes as he continued speaking.

"My grandparents always told me that anger couldn't fix these things, that stuff like that could only be fixed with love. I hated hearing that. I felt like they were saying my mom and me couldn't be fixed, because my mom didn't love me. I started getting into trouble. Pops and Nana sat me down again and again and tried to get through to me, but I didn't want to hear any of it.

"Finally, one day, I was eating dinner with Nana. I don't remember where Pops was, but I remember that it was just her and me. And she asked me to just try to love my mom." Kem grimaced. "I tried to be smart, asked her how me being a sap would do anything to get Mom to shape up and act like an adult. Nana told me I couldn't change who my mom was or how she lived her life. Only she could do that. But I could change how I lived my life. I didn't have to spend my life hurting myself and other people with my anger."

Kem pressed his lips together and shook his head, taking a minute before he went on. "It had never occurred to my stupid, egocentric self that I was hurting anyone else. But I could see right then that I was making Nana miserable, that I caused her just as much worry as her daughter did. So I told her I'd try."

Kem took another drink of cocoa, then handed it back to Sera and looked her straight in the eyes. "It was like walking out of a cave. All the heavy anger I'd carried around for so long started to get lighter. I started to see the humor in things again. Found things that I enjoyed. And I could see people better. I mean, not literally, but I looked at my grandparents and understood them better. I looked at my friends at school and could see things going on under the surface. It didn't make any difference with my mom, not at first, but it made all the difference for me. And then—" His voice caught, and he cleared his throat. "Mom's still not an award-winning parent or anything, but she came for Christmas last year. I hadn't spent Christmas with my mom for over twenty years."

Sera sat quietly, prodding the hot coal of hurt that had burned in a corner of her heart since she was nine years old. "He left us," she said softly.

"I know." Kem spoke with a fervent empathy that pierced Sera's heart. "But now you're here, and he's here. Doesn't it seem like a fair chance to do some healing? Maybe find out why he left?"

"I'm not sure I want to know." Sera choked back the fear that had lingered in the back of her mind since she was nine years old, that she had done something wrong, that she had somehow been too obnoxious, too nosy, too *something* that had driven her brother away. Her disastrous first boyfriend had been enough to show her that she was only dateable for creeps. She didn't think she could handle learning for certain that Langdon's long absence had been somehow her fault.

Kem reached out and touched her hand. "Give it a chance, Sera," he said, a strain of pleading in his voice. "Don't leave yet. Give it some time."

As if he'd realized what he was doing, Kem snatched his hand back. Still, Sera's skin buzzed where he'd touched her. *Stop,* she told her erratically beating heart, firmly and completely in vain. *You're the one who made him swear a friendship pact. You don't get to run away with any ridiculous ideas. He wouldn't want you anyway, not after your nutbag display that first day.*

Taking a deep breath, Sera said, "How do I love someone I haven't seen for twelve years? I can't just tell my heart what to do." *It's obviously not listening to me right now.*

Kem shrugged. "Loving someone isn't just a feeling. It's listening, watching, helping, understanding. It's making someone feel seen. And being loved like that can change a person. It changed me. I wouldn't be where I am right now without Nana and Pops loving all the fight out of me."

He grinned, a wry, lopsided grin that deepened one dimple. Sera felt her stomach flip, and she looked away, trying to hide the smile that sprang onto her face in response. Her eyes landed on the empty soup bowl.

How much had Kem done for her since she came here? Between supplying cocoa on demand, showing her around the town, and making every effort to make her feel at home here, he'd shown her more kindness than she could have hoped for. From the beginning, he'd made her feel seen.

Why had she been stupid enough to swear him to a friendship-only pact?

"I'll stay," she said, forcing her voice to stay calm in spite of her heart racing rebelliously. "For now. And…I'll try what you said about loving." Heat rushed through her cheeks, and she hastily added, "Loving Langdon, I mean." Cripes, could she get any more obvious? She didn't dare look directly at Kem, but she could see his eyes crinkle from the edge of her vision. Was he laughing at her? Or maybe he had missed her overeager specification and was just smiling because he was glad for her. Or maybe he just thought she was a total dork.

"I'll take your dishes down," Kem said, reaching over Sera to pick up her bowl and the thermos. Sera very conscientiously did *not* focus on how he smelled of pine trees and pastries. It was perfectly logical he should smell that amazing, given that he lived in a mountain village and worked as a pastry chef.

"Thanks," Sera said, realizing in a sudden wave that her muscles were worn from a day of walking and her eyes itched with exhaustion. She dragged herself up off the floor with an effort and turned to Kem. "Thanks for everything."

"Hey, that's what friends are for."

For a second, Sera wanted to throw her arms around him and hug him, dishes and all. But she hesitated too long, and the moment passed. Kem left the room with a cheery, "Get a good night's sleep!"

Sera let the door swing closed, then pushed it open a crack and watched Kem walk down the hall to the back stairs. Once he'd disappeared down to the kitchen, she leaned her head against the doorjamb.

You were the one who insisted on being just friends, she told herself sternly. *It's your own darn fault, Seraphina. Don't let your heart run away with you when you've already walled him out.*

But she had the sneaking suspicion that all the stern talking to herself in the world couldn't change how she felt like all the lights dimmed as soon as Kem left the room.

STARLING CHRISTMAS FESTIVAL
(8 DAYS UNTIL CHRISTMAS)

The sun was barely peeking over the horizon when Langdon left his house and walked to the town square. Soon enough, the square would be crowded with most of the town's inhabitants and guests for the tree-trimming festivities. But now, with the temperature hovering in the teens and only the barest sliver of sun showing, the square was deserted. Langdon tugged his scarf up to cover the lower half of his face and tugged his hat down to keep his ears from freezing off. The temperature was much too low for sitting on a bench and having a good think, so instead Langdon went to the enormous tree in the very center of the square and walked in a slow circle around it.

"I thought I might find you here." Felicity's voice drifted through the empty morning air.

Looking up at her, Langdon smiled wearily. "I couldn't spend another minute tossing and turning in bed."

Felicity slipped her arm into his, and they took a couple of circles around the tree in silence. Somehow, having Felicity there untangled the knots of worry that had kept him up all night and turned them into words.

"What if they don't want me back?" he asked abruptly.

Felicity rubbed his arm gently, taking a moment before she responded. "You can't control what your family feels or does, Langdon. And I don't know them, so I can't pretend to have any idea of how they'll react. But I've worked with Sera for two weeks. And looking back on that time, I'm coming to realize why her account and her personality spoke to me so profoundly."

Felicity tugged on Langdon's arm. He looked down at her, reading the determination in her eyes and loving every ounce of it.

"She reminded me of you," Felicity said simply. "When she got here, she understood the inn right away. She knew exactly what made it so charming and how to show it off. I think the two of you are cut from the same cloth. And I wonder if she's just as afraid of rejection as you are."

They walked in silence for another lap, then Felicity pulled her arm free. "Come on back to the inn. Breakfast will be going soon."

"I've got a bagel." *And I'm terrified of running into my baby sister.* "I'm going to hang around and make sure everything gets running smoothly."

Felicity sighed. "Okay. Don't freeze, okay? I'll bring you some cocoa in a little while."

Impulsively, Langdon pulled her back and kissed her, the

50

warmth of her lips spreading through his veins. When they broke apart, he held her tightly, then released her with a sigh. "Thanks for not leaving me," he said softly. "I'd have understood if you hated me."

"Langdon," Felicity said, shaking her head. Her eyes sparkled with a sheen of tears. "You're too hard on yourself. I love you, now more than ever. And we're going to get through this together. But first, we're going to trim a tree."

Sera woke the next morning from a deep sleep that went into her bones. She still had the blanket Kem had wrapped around her shoulders the night before. Burrowing deep into its fleecy warmth, she sighed. A solid night's sleep had done wonders, and the tiniest gleam of optimism sprouted in her heart.

The kitchen buzzed with activity when she went down, chefs shouting back and forth over the clanging of pots and the beeping of ovens. The tall racks were bursting with pastries, even more than usual. And Kem was already there, whisking something steaming in a tall pot. He winked at her from across the room, then jumped back into action, tossing this and that into the pot, rolling out dough, whisking and kneading and stirring.

Grabbing a chocolate croissant from one of the racks, Sera ducked out of the busy kitchen and into the dining room. A surprising number of people were there, considering the early hour. Sera caught sight of Felicity hurrying out the front door with a box exploding with tinsel.

Of course! The community Christmas festival. With everything else going on, Sera had completely forgotten the event. Holding her camera bag so it wouldn't bang against her side, Sera ran after Felicity.

"Do you need help carrying anything out?" she asked.

Felicity glanced at her, then did a double-take. Smiling, she said, "I've got this. Glad to see you here, though. Today's a great day for pictures. And thankfully, the snow has let up for now." Setting the box down next to a pile of others, Felicity flapped a hand at Sera. "Go enjoy yourself!"

Sera took her at her word, heading down the road toward the quilt shop. A grandmotherly woman was setting out bolts of fabric in the shape of a Christmas tree. Hovering back a bit, Sera pulled out her camera and snapped a few shots of the woman working with a satisfied smile.

All up and down the street, businesses set up their booths, calling back and forth to each other and laughing over stories from tree trimmings long past. Sera's heart filled at the happiness electrifying the mountain air. She worked her way back up the road to the enormous Christmas tree in the town square. A tall ladder had been set up, and Felicity handed strands of tinsel to the man standing at the top of it. Langdon.

A funny jolt went through Sera's stomach. She still hadn't gotten used to the fact that her long-lost brother was *right here*, where she might see him at any moment. For a second, she was tempted to move on, hurry past.

Instead, she lifted her camera. A wide shot of the people

working on the tree. A close-up of the tinsel sparkling on the boughs. And then she turned the lens on her brother, catching the laugh that came when Felicity said something funny, the careful placement of the tinsel, the moment he nearly fell off the ladder and got a good scolding from below.

Sera had to turn away after that, crossing to the far side of the street and continuing uphill. Her brother seemed happy here. Was that fair? For him to find happiness when he'd abandoned them all?

Was it fair for her to wish that he hadn't been happy? She didn't, not really. That free, open laugh she'd seen just now— she didn't remember seeing that at home. Her memories of him weren't always the clearest, but she mostly remembered him as quiet, serious, withdrawn. It lightened her, somehow, to see him smile that way. For so long, she had eavesdropped on her parents' conversations about whether Langdon was safe, whether he had food, whether he had a friend to help him. The quiet little knots Sera had tied in her stomach through all those conversations loosened now, seeing her brother safe, well, and happy.

Maybe Kem was right. Maybe it was possible to love someone she hadn't seen in twelve years. But loving was one thing, and forgiving was quite another.

Sighing, Sera tried to let go of her nagging thoughts and enjoy the Christmas atmosphere. She went back to the inn and helped carry out trays of pastries to sit beside a giant vat of hot chocolate. Kem was still frantically mixing, pouring, and baking, so she went back out to the street, where the festivities were now getting underway.

Kids whooshed down hills on everything from wooden toboggans to plastic discs to cardboard boxes, sometimes coming close enough to a booth to draw stern shouts from the booth owners. Guests from the inn flooded out into the street, joined by visitors from nearby towns whose cars lined the sloping road down below the town. Sera snapped photos of tourists trying on hats, community members hanging red and silver ornaments on the tree, and toddlers with chocolate-smeared faces.

A call went up for all the kids to gather behind the inn for snow olympics. Sera followed the flow of kids, sure to get some winning shots no matter what kind of games they had planned. Kids and snow were a priceless combination.

Behind the inn, next to the huge, gorgeous oak tree that stood sentinel over the building, three squares had been tramped into the snow. The square in the middle had been shoveled, the snow tossed into the squares on either side in two massive piles. Langdon stood in that middle square, sticking his fingers in his mouth to whistle for everyone's attention. Sera covered her ears just as his piercing whistle split the air, loud enough to shock the whole crowd into silence. She grinned at some of the kids wincing and rubbing their ears. She remembered all too well what Langdon's whistle could do to the unsuspecting.

"Listen up!" he called, totally superfluously. He'd gotten everyone's attention. "Here in the middle, we've got snowman races." He pointed to a pile of burlap bags painted white with black dots for snowman buttons. "On that side, you can build your own snow fort. Be sure to keep a pile of snowballs on hand to defend it! And over here is our snowman building contest. Or snow woman, or snow animal. Whatever inspires you. Pick your square and get to it!"

The kids cheered and ran, nearly knocking over several adults in their hurry. Sera circled the squares with her camera. Some kids darted from square to square, while others went to work with a dedication that would have impressed Michelangelo. The kids racing in the burlap bags ranged from game-faced and determined to kids laughing so hard they could barely hop. Four kids had banded together to build a snow fort of epic proportions. And some girl in the snowman square had obviously been reading Calvin and Hobbes.

And through it all was Langdon. He went from judging the races to jumping in his own bag, clowning around and falling on the frozen grass every other step. He lobbed easy snowballs at the snow forts and got pelted in return. In the snowman square, he tried again and again to balance a huge snow head on a skinny snow body, scratching his head among peals of laughter every time it fell off or collapsed the tiny body. When he finally made it work, all the kids cheered.

"He's the one who started all this, you know." Felicity appeared at Sera's elbow without warning.

Sera glanced at her. "The snow olympics?"

"The tree trimming. Bringing the whole town out to celebrate together. He's struggled with Christmas for years. It's his favorite holiday, but it's also the day he remembers most that he's on his own."

"By his own choice," Sera said defensively.

Felicity tilted her head. "Maybe. But that doesn't make it any easier. He's tried to fill up that missing piece of his heart with the people here. And even though he's found places in his heart for all these people, none of them quite fit in that family-shaped hole."

Sera snapped a few more pictures, chewing on Felicity's words. Lowering the camera, she asked, "What about you? Are you going home for Christmas?"

Felicity's face tightened with quiet pain. "The year I went to college, my parents and my little brother came to pick me up and take me home for Christmas. The roads were bad, and they spun out on the freeway, right in front of a semi." She blinked and looked back at Langdon. "I love your brother with all my heart. I know you've been hurt, and I don't blame you. But I know what it is to live without family. And now I know that he doesn't have to. Please help him. He wants to go home, he just doesn't know how."

Doesn't know how? Sera stared at her brother, now lying on the ground behind an abandoned fort and lobbing snowballs at an army of kids. She had never considered that Langdon might be afraid to return home. Why would he? Didn't he know how much their parents ached for even the slightest hint of news from him?

No, she realized. He hadn't been there to see Mom painstakingly scouring the internet for him, or Dad's temper broken with regrets. For the first time, Sera wondered if Langdon hadn't left because he hated them all. What if he'd felt like he couldn't come home?

Kem's cheerful voice cut into her thoughts. "Frozen your fingers off yet?"

Sera smiled even before she saw the steaming cup of cocoa he'd brought her. "You've saved me from frostbite once again," she said, taking the cocoa. Felicity squeezed her arm and melted away into the crowd.

"How are you doing?" Kem asked quietly, looking over at Langdon.

Sera considered the question as she watched her oldest brother charge a massive snow fort. From the inn came distant strains of Christmas carols singing from the strings of a violin, completing the holiday scene.

"You know," Sera said, "for the first time in a really long time, I think things are going to turn out okay."

Riveting Reading
(7 days until Christmas)

The rest of that day and the next was a whirl of activity, in the aftermath of the tree trimming and the start of Christmas crowds flooding into the inn. Felicity told Sera they were completely booked over Christmas, something that had never happened before. Sera and Langdon crossed paths more often as they spent less effort avoiding each other. They didn't speak much, but, Sera thought, at least they were getting used to seeing each other. That had to count for something.

The evening after the tree trimming, after Sera had eaten dinner and before Kem was done in the kitchen, Sera wandered up to the third floor. Several of the private dining rooms were in use that evening, but one on the end stood empty. With a quick glance around to be sure no one was watching, Sera slipped inside.

With curiosity pushing at her, Sera hesitated for only a second before climbing up onto the chair she'd stacked on the table.

Climbing through the floor, not the ceiling, she reminded herself as a bout of vertigo threatened. Straightening slowly, she pushed the panel out of the way and pulled herself into the attic.

After her last trip to the attic, Sera had attached a tiny flashlight to her keychain. She turned it on now and made her way over to the lone box in the corner. Pulling a letter out, she paused.

These were written by Langdon, apparently without any intention of someone else reading them. There was no knowing what he said in them. And once she read them, there would be no unreading them.

But she had to know whether what Felicity said was true. Taking a steadying breath, she pulled out one from the middle. It was dated April 4, six years earlier.

Mom, Dad, Elliot, Rhett, and Phina,

I bought an inn today. You wouldn't believe what happened leading up to it. I can't even believe it. I wasn't planning on sinking my savings into a broken-down building in the middle of nowhere, but now that it's done, I'd never go back. It's an incredible building, and when it's polished up some, it'll really shine. Someone told me no one else could fix up this inn the way I could. That's a load of crap, but I'm going to try not to disappoint them. Maybe someday you'll see it. Stranger things have happened. Just today, in fact.

I'm sorry for everything. I miss you.

Langdon

Sera blinked back an excess of moisture in her eyes and pulled out the next envelope.

Mom,

I don't know what I've done. This inn needs so much work. I've never done a project this big. I'm starting to think I'll be the only one who ever steps through that front door. But somehow, I still don't regret buying it. I've spent my whole life doing things for other people, and this is the first thing I've done just because I wanted to. It's mine, and it doesn't matter if it lives up to anyone else's expectations.

Who am I kidding? I'm always trying to live up to someone else's expectations. Maybe someday I'll stop falling on my face.

I'm sorry for everything. I miss you.

Langdon

Sera went through a few more. Some were addressed to the whole family, some just to Mom. Almost all of them were short. Sometimes they were hopeful, sometimes despondent. He always signed off the same way. *I'm sorry for everything. I miss you.*

The sixth one Sera pulled out was fatter than the others. She extracted a few sheets of paper, folded with sharp creases, and flattened them out.

Dad, this one started. Sera's breath caught, sensing that this was one different from all the others. It had to be. Twelve years later, her stomach still curled at the memory of that last phone call between her dad and Langdon.

"What are you doing?"

Sera dropped her flashlight with a gasp. Langdon's head protruded from the attic floor. He lifted a lantern into the space, hoisted himself up, and took in the scene. The letters lay around Sera, opened and scattered, silently condemning her. As Langdon's expression darkened, Sera got the distinct feeling that this had been an awful idea.

"Those are private," Langdon said, his voice deadly quiet. "And you're not supposed to be sneaking around up here. Get out."

Deep inside, Sera knew she was in the wrong. She shouldn't have gone prying. But being caught, reprimanded, and kicked out by the brother she was trying hard to love set her off. "I'm just trying to get to know you," she snapped. "Maybe if you'd called once in a while, I wouldn't have to sneak to do it."

"Get to know me? Or try to rescue my wayward soul?" Langdon snatched the letter out of Sera's hand. "I'm happy here, okay? Maybe I didn't finish college. Maybe I don't have some snazzy job where I wear a suit and tie every day. But I don't need that."

Sera flushed. "And I guess you don't need your family either, huh?"

"I've done just fine on my own."

The words hit Sera like a slap. Shooting to her feet, she stormed to the hole in the floor, skirting wide around Langdon for fear that if she got too close she'd kick him. Sitting on the edge of the hole, she looked up for a second, her heart pounding a furious beat.

"I wish I'd never applied for this job," she said, choking on her anger. "I wish I'd left you here on your own, just how you want."

Dropping through the hole in the floor, she hopped off the chair and vanished into the hallway.

Langdon stood in the middle of his scattered letters. They were precisely why he'd come up here. For once, he had started to think he would be able to tell his family all the things he'd been stashing away for so many years. The magic of the tree trimming had fooled him into thinking he could change the way he'd lived for over a decade.

And now he'd wrecked it. In one burst of temper, he'd ruined his second chance.

Slowly, mechanically, he gathered the letters, glancing over them to see what Sera had found. He paused, scanning the one he'd written the day he bought the inn.

Maybe someday you'll see it.

Ha. Langdon crumpled the paper and threw it into the box, then tossed the other ones in without bothering to stuff them back in the envelopes. Closing up the box, he sat beside it and pressed his palms against his eyes, blocking out the light from his lantern.

In the darkness, his mind went to Felicity. She had swept in on opening night and instantly become an essential part of the inn. And, by extension, an essential part of him. Langdon had fought it for years before finally relenting and trying to make himself worthy of her. He'd done all he could to ensure her happiness, to heal the scars left by her family's sudden deaths, to be half the support to her that she'd been to him.

If she still wanted to marry him after this fiasco, his family wouldn't just be his anymore. It would be hers. And she deserved the chance to meet them, to have some semblance of the family she'd missed for so long.

He'd been unable to repair his relationship with his family with only himself for motivation, not when he felt himself so unworthy of coming back to them. But for Felicity's sake, he would do whatever it took to fix his mistakes.

Taking a deep breath, Langdon took the box of letters and lifted it carefully down into the private dining room. He replaced the panel, put the room back in order, and carried the box down the back stairs and into the kitchen.

Crowded as the kitchen was, he saw Sera the second he walked in. She looked up from the bowl of brownie batter she was stirring and froze, misery spreading across her face. Beside her, Kem put a hand on her elbow. Langdon forced his legs to move, carrying him across the kitchen and over to where his sister stood watching him like an approaching rattlesnake.

"Phina, can I talk with you for a second?" Langdon had been trying to call her Sera for days and couldn't get past how wrong it sounded in his mouth. Maybe she didn't go by Phina anymore, but it felt more authentic to him, and all he wanted right now was to get her to *see* him.

"Sure." Sera's response was flat and dull. She didn't move, waiting expectantly by the brownie batter while Kem looked on and the other chefs snuck curious glances their direction.

"In Felicity's office," Langdon clarified, glancing around meaningfully.

For a second, he thought Sera was going to refuse him and make some fine gossip among the kitchen crew. But then she left her brownie batter and led the way out of the kitchen, through the dining room, and behind the grand staircase to Felicity's office. She folded her arms as Langdon unlocked the door, and she crossed her legs tightly when they went inside and sat down.

Maybe he should have given her more time. Her body language was direct and pointed, and Langdon already felt like he'd been speared. *For Felicity,* he reminded himself, and cleared his throat.

But before he could speak, Sera uncrossed her legs and said, "I shouldn't have been reading your private letters. I'm sorry. I really was just trying to figure you out."

She sounded brusque, but not insincere. "I'm sorry, too," Langdon said, the words sapping him. "I shouldn't have lost my temper."

Sera nodded. And then...they sat. Silence stretched on second after second. Langdon searched his mind in a panic. He'd apologized. *She'd* apologized, which he hadn't expected. Wasn't this the part where they made up and things got better between them? But what did you say after the apologies? Was he supposed to talk about himself? The inn? Or ask about the family? Family. Definitely family.

But just as he opened his mouth to ask, Sera stood and said, "I should get back to the kitchen. I'm helping Kem with the dessert bar tonight."

"Oh." Langdon cursed his slow brain for failing to come up with a better response than that. "Okay. Thanks for doing that.

And for everything else you've done. Felicity was right to hire you."

Sera paused right next to the door and looked back at him. He couldn't read her expression—expectation? Uncertainty? Before he could decide, she left.

Langdon dropped his head between his knees, his heart crumpling like a piece of tin foil. He'd failed. Again.

***

"That's the last of them," Kem said an hour later, dusting the final brownie with powdered sugar. He set it on the tray to be taken out to the dessert bar. "What do you say we get out of here?"

Sera nodded, taking a slow breath in and out again. "I'd like that."

"Great. I think the fireplace at Marty's is calling our names."

After running upstairs for her coat and hat, Sera met Kem at the front door of the inn and walked out into the frigid air.

It had snowed on and off throughout the day, but the clouds had cleared out for the night. Stars reflected brightly off the fresh white powder. Tourists still straggled along the main street, but all people-sounds were muted by nature's thick blanket. Lifting her face to the sky, Sera filled her lungs with icy air.

"I lied," she said suddenly.

Kem raised an eyebrow at her. "When?"

"When I was mad at Langdon. I told him I wished I'd never come here. It's not true. There's something healing in this place. It's beautiful, and the people are good. If I'd never come Starling, I'd never have seen those stars dancing up there like no one's watching. I wouldn't have the confidence that my hobby could be useful in a decent career. And I wouldn't have met—"

Sera turned to look at Kem, and the words caught up in her throat. His hazel eyes bored into her, waiting with breathtaking intensity for her to finish her sentence. *Friendship pact,* Sera thought weakly. But a much larger part of her was chanting, *Pact, schmact. Go for it.*

"I wouldn't have met you," she finished defiantly.

Kem's dimples deepened. "I'm glad you're here, too," he said, his smile so big his eyes scrunched. Holding out a gentlemanly arm, he said, "Shall we?"

She took his arm. They walked slowly down the icy, sloped street, slipping here and there and keeping each other upright. Once they made it inside the warmth of Marty's cafe, Kem took Sera's coat and hung it up for her. "Go grab us a place by the fire," he said, nodding toward the collection of chairs and couches clustered around the fireplace. "I'll get the food."

Nodding, Sera walked to the fireplace, stretching her hands out to warm up as she sized up the available seats. Her instinct was to go for the individual chairs. Safer that way. Especially given that her sensibility seemed to have been rocked by the evening's events.

But her eyes kept straying to the empty loveseat nearby. Her head was full of the way Kem had looked at her, so intensely hopeful, and the sensation of his arm holding hers securely.

Before she could lose her nerve, she stepped over to the loveseat and sat down. Kem joined her a minute later, setting two cocoas and a bag of chocolate-drizzled popcorn on the coffee table next to the couch.

"So do you want to talk about why Mr. Hyatt looked more uncomfortable than a pig on a porcupine, or just pretend it never happened?" Kem asked, sitting rather closer to the center of the couch than the end.

"A pig on a porcupine?" Sera laughed. "Do you spend your days coming up with ridiculous imagery to slip into conversation?"

Kem grinned. "No. I spend my days coming up with ways to make you laugh. And it's well worth the effort."

A heat entirely unrelated to the fire spread through Sera's cheeks. She reached for her cocoa to cover it. "I went back up to the attic," she confessed. "That box—it's full of letters Langdon wrote to our family, but never sent. I wanted to understand why, so I decided to go read them for myself."

"What was in them?" Kem asked, his eyes alight with curiosity.

Sera swirled the cocoa around in her cup. "A lot of regrets. He wrote things that were going on in his everyday life, but always with this edge, this expectation that no one would care. Or that someone would be disappointed in him. At the end of every letter, he'd write, 'I'm sorry for everything.'"

Kem gave a low whistle. "Sad."

"Right? And then, just as I was starting to get him, he caught me."

"Noooo," Kem groaned, slapping a hand over his eyes.

"Yes. And he was *mad*. He told me to get out and said he didn't need me, that he was perfectly happy on his own without any family." Saying it out loud pricked Sera's heart all over again. She swallowed and stared into the fire, watching the reds, oranges, and yellows dancing around each other in a mesmerizing flicker.

A large, warm hand covered hers. Sera stiffened, not daring to look at Kem, not trusting herself to move, keeping her eyes on the flames as if they might give her an answer of what to do next. She'd spent so long guarding herself against this kind of thing that she knew this was the moment she should pull away; otherwise, judging by the way her breath was caught in her chest, she'd give in.

The thing was, giving in sounded pretty good.

"From what you've said about his letters," Kem said, not moving his hand, "I don't think he meant that."

Sera nodded slowly, her heart racing. Then, turning her hand over, she laced her fingers through his. "I think he and I both have a bad habit of saying things we don't mean."

Out of the corner of her eye, she watched Kem's eyes squinch up in a smile again. "You have no idea how glad I am to hear that," he said with a relieved sigh. "I didn't know what kind of torture I was getting myself into when I swore we wouldn't be anything but friends."

"Torture?" Sera laughed. "Hardly."

"Yes, torture." Lifting his free hand to her cheek, Kem turned her to face him. Sera leaned into the warmth of his palm, her stomach fluttering at the closeness she'd fought for so long. Kem's eyes pulled her in, enveloping her, as he said, "I wasn't lying when I said I was just looking for a friend. That was all I expected to find. But then you turned out to be not just someone I could have a laugh with, but someone I could talk to, someone I could trust. I've never told anyone about my mom, but I didn't think twice about talking through it with you. It just made sense. And seeing you struggle to come to terms with your brother being here—every time you hurt, I hurt. I couldn't sleep the night you first saw him and ran off in such a panic. That was the first time I realized how much you meant to me. And I've only realized it more every day. Seraphina, I…"

He trailed off, and Sera realized how much closer they'd gotten. Had he moved? Had she? He was close enough for her to smell his distinctive pine-and-sugar scent, and she couldn't pull away from it. There were inches between them. No, an inch. Maybe half an inch.

With a quick, longing moan, Kem closed the gap and kissed her, his hand sliding from her cheek to the back of her neck. Sera lost herself in the moment, weaving her fingers into his curly black hair, the walls she'd carefully built up around her heart melting like chocolate on a hot stove.

Until, with a sharp jab from her head to her heart, Sera realized what she was doing. She pulled back with a gasp, panic shooting away all the warmth of Kem's touch. Kem scooted back, his eyes wide.

"Sera," he said, fear cutting through his eyes. "That was…fast. I'm sorry. I just—I don't want to scare you off. I'm sorry."

"No," Sera said, not even sure what she was saying no to as a torrent of painful memories broke loose. "No, it's not—it's okay.

I'm not—I'm sorry. It's me. I just...I need to go." She stood up, then made the mistake of looking back at Kem's anguished face. What was she doing? This was Kem. He wasn't going to hurt her.

But now she'd hurt him.

"I'm sorry," she whispered, then fled out into the snow, not even stopping to grab her coat. A biting wind cut through her shirt. She ran up the hill, slipping once on the ice and going down hard on her knee. Staggering back to her feet, she limped the rest of the way to the inn. Going up the porch steps, she checked over her shoulder to make sure Kem wasn't following her—and promptly collided with someone. Her foot slipped, and she nearly went backwards off the steps she'd just climbed. But before she could fall, two hands grabbed her shoulders and pulled her back into balance.

"Thank you," she murmured, looking up. Instantly, her heart sank even further. Langdon frowned down at her, his hands tight around her shoulders. *Just what I needed to finish off the night.*

"Am I about to hire a new pastry chef?" Langdon growled.

The question was so unexpected that Sera couldn't form a response. Without ever letting go, Langdon steered her inside, through the lobby, and back to Felicity's empty office. Sera was too bewildered to resist. After guiding her to a seat, Langdon pulled another chair up in front of her and sat with his elbows on his knees.

"I may be the world's worst older brother," he said, his voice a low, threatening rumble, "but I'm not about to stand by and let some snotfaced sweets chef take liberties with my baby sister. What did he do to you?"

Sera's face burned three shades of red. "Nothing! He didn't do anything wrong, I swear."

Langdon sat back and gripped the arms of his chair, his knuckles turning white. "Seraphina Hyatt. I just found you out in the snow with not so much as a jacket, running for your life and looking over your shoulder. And I know perfectly well who you were with. He'll be lucky if firing him is all I do. I've got a good hammer that's taken down a wall or two in this place."

After what she'd just done, Kem didn't need his boss coming after him with a hammer. "Shut up and listen, Lang," Sera said, desperate to defend the innocent. "Kem didn't do anything. I just…I freaked out. I haven't let myself think of anyone that way since I took a textbook to the face."

Langdon's grip loosened, his eyebrows rising in a startled leap. "What?"

Sera swallowed hard, blinking away the obnoxious burning of tears in her eyes. "It's…stupid. This guy I dated in college. It was three years ago, but…he seemed like he cared, but the longer it went on, the more it felt like a bear trap instead of a relationship."

"How so?" Langdon's fierce anger had settled into a fierce gentleness, a strange combination that bolstered Sera in revisiting one of the worst years of her life. She took a moment to gather her strength, then plunged on.

"He'd get angry if I spent my free time with anyone else, even a study group. I couldn't be me, couldn't do anything I enjoyed without worrying whether it would set him off. I tried to break up with him, but he kept reeling me back in with twisted words

71

and apologies and promises. Sometimes threats." Sera cringed. "I didn't know how to get away. Until he threw a textbook at me for saying hello to a guy in one of my classes. It cracked my cheekbone."

The pain, the anger, the humiliation flooded through her, beating against her weary soul. Sera covered the left side of her face and shuddered. "I told the nurses what had happened. He didn't go to jail. I transferred to a different university and swore I'd never be stupid enough to get stuck in that again."

Langdon let out a slow sigh. "Felicity mentioned you were a little jumpy around Kem the first day. She wondered if something had happened."

Groaning, Sera said, "I felt like such an idiot. He was being so sweet, and I was awful to him. At least, until he swore he was only looking to be a friend. I believed him, and I believed that was all I wanted, too. At first, I didn't want to get too close because I was scared I'd end up with another book in the face. Or worse. I was afraid if I had to go through another relationship like that, he'd break me this time, that I wouldn't be able to walk away." Sera covered her face. "But the longer I spent with him, the more worried I was that I would never be good enough for him. That I could never put away the things I've been through, that I'd never get back to who I was, to enough *normal* to have a decent relationship. And I proved it tonight."

Slumping in her chair, Sera confessed, "He kissed me. I wanted him to, and he did, and it was wonderful. And then my head ran away with me, telling me that because he kissed me, he'd think he owned me. That he'd say I owed him. That this dream would turn into a nightmare all over again." She kicked her heel against the chair in frustration. "I know Kem isn't like that. But I ran away anyway, and now I've ruined everything. I hurt him."

Sera stared up at the ceiling, lost in her misery. She was so far gone in her own thoughts that it startled her when Langdon put a hand on her knee.

"I'm going to tell you a story," Langdon said, shifting his weight with a vulnerable expression. "The first time I met Felicity, it was the night the inn opened. She was three days late because a snowstorm had grounded her flight. I had been up all night making the final preparations for the grand opening. Mrs. Warble had spent I don't know how many hours on the cake for the evening. Felicity showed up an hour before go time, apologizing for getting stuck in an airport for days. She was already dressed for the party, this gorgeous dark blue dress with a white sash." Grimacing, Langdon said, "I was a wreck. Even though it was totally not her fault, I lost my cool and started to chew her out for not showing up when she'd promised to. I took a step toward her as Mrs. Warble carried the cake past me into the room. My foot went just the wrong place and tripped her, and she dropped the cake right on top of Felicity."

"No," Sera breathed, a small smile breaking through.

"Yes. It was literally from head to toe. I'm not sure which of the three of us was the most horrified." Langdon laughed quietly. "That's part of the reason we hired Kem. Mrs. Warble refused to make desserts for me after that fiasco. I couldn't look Felicity in the face for days. It took me years to admit to myself that I was head over heels for her, and another year after that before I got the guts to ask her out. And somehow, she still agreed to marry me." Langdon shook his head, as if he still couldn't fathom it.

"You know, that's almost as bad as the first time Elliott brought a girlfriend home from college," Sera said, her grin growing at the memory. "Maybe twenty minutes after she walked in the door, Rhett chipped her tooth with a ping-pong paddle."

Langdon laughed again, louder this time. The sound went straight to Sera's heart, soothing its rawness. For the first time, she truly felt like she had her brother back.

"Phina, if your pathetic brothers can manage to hold onto a relationship, you'll be just fine," Langdon said, nudging her foot with his. "I can't imagine what you've gone through. I've seen you around the inn, though, and I can tell you—you're resilient, and you're strong." His voice lowered as his gaze fell to the floor. "Stronger than I am."

Sera studied his face, stitching together what she'd seen of him and what she'd read in his letters. Softly and cautiously, hoping she wouldn't scare him away, she asked, "Why didn't you ever come home?"

The words struck him, made him flinch. His chin dipped farther down to his chest. "I—I didn't plan to. I mean, I didn't plan not to. But when it came time, I was afraid. A coward." Self-derision dripped from his tone. "I kept telling myself I'd go home, or I'd call home, or I'd text. But every time I tried, I didn't have the words. Everything I planned to say got drowned out by knowing that it would never be enough to make up for everything I'd done wrong. And the longer it went, the more pathetic my excuses became. In the end, it was easier to just stop trying. I convinced myself you were better off if I stayed out of your lives."

A painful lump lodged in Sera's throat. All these years, she'd been so angry with Langdon for choosing to stay away. She'd never imagined he felt like he didn't belong there anymore.

"You know," she said, her voice just a touch shaky, "after you… after Dad…well, Dad still hasn't forgiven himself. He tells us he loves us so often it's kind of annoying. But Mom told me once, he says it so much to us because he can't say it to you. He's trying to compensate, because he wants to tell you he loves you so badly." A thought—an impossible, bright, glorious, ridiculous thought— jumped into Sera's mind. Before it could flit away, along with her nerves, Sera said, "Langdon, come home for Christmas."

Langdon's head jerked up. Sera tried to read the expression in his eyes. Hope, so much hope it broke her heart. But after a second, fear and doubt clouded over the hope, and he shook his head. "No. Not at Christmas. I can't. Going home would be hard enough without…"

"Without what? Twinkling lights and Christmas spirit? Langdon, Mom still hangs up your stocking every year. Mom *fills* your stocking every year. Just in case you come home. Do you know what it would mean to her to have you there to open it?"

He swallowed and blinked hard. "But what about everyone else?"

"What about everyone else? We all want you home, Langdon.

We've wanted you home for twelve years. We just didn't know where to find you."

She could see him weakening, but he still protested. "But… the inn…"

"Can survive without you and Felicity for a few days."

Langdon's eyes lit up. "You think it would be okay to bring Felicity?"

Sera snorted. "Langdon. The only thing that would make Mom happier than you coming home for Christmas would be you coming home with a girl."

Langdon laughed, but the unease hadn't completely left his posture. He shifted in his seat. "You weren't all that happy to see me when we first ran into each other here. What if Rhett and Elliott aren't either? I don't want to ruin everybody's Christmas."

"Stop it with the self-martyrdom," Sera said bluntly. "I wasn't happy because you called me an idiot for not wanting to stay at the inn over Christmas. I don't know how Rhett and Elliott are going to respond. It's probably not going to be perfectly easy. It's been twelve years. But it's not going to get any easier until you take the first step."

Standing, Langdon crossed the room and stood by the window, looking out at the snow-covered old oak. Sera bit her lip and forced herself to wait patiently while he thought. *He's not going to do it,* she thought, her heart sinking as she looked at his frown, his furrowed brow.

After two long minutes, Langdon turned back. "Okay."

Sera's heart leaped. "Okay?"

He took a deep breath. "I'll come."

The words bounced around in Sera's ears for a moment before settling in. Leaping to her feet, she bounded across the room and hugged him fiercely. Langdon lifted his arms to hover uncertainly for a second. He hugged her back, cautiously at first, then tightly.

"Thank you, Langdon," Sera said, her voice thick with emotion.

He cleared his throat. "Just one thing," he said, his own voice shaky. "Don't—don't tell Mom and Dad. I want to see them face to face. The phone didn't go so well last time."

Sera winced. "Dad won't yell at you. I promise."

"I know." He didn't know, not for sure. Sera could see the wariness in his eyes. "Just do that for me, okay?"

"Okay." Sera broke out in a yawn, and Langdon squeezed her shoulder.

"Go get some rest."

She looked down. "I should go find Kem and apologize."

"I'm sure he's gone home already, and you'll both do better in the morning with some space and some sleep."

Sera sighed. "You're probably right."

"It does happen on occasion." Langdon smiled. "You can't save the entire world in one night, Phina."

"I guess." Sera tilted her head to look up at him. "I'm glad Felicity hired me."

Langdon laughed and brushed at his eyes. "Me too, kid. Now go to bed before you turn me into a leaky faucet."

Sera hugged him again, then walked out through the late-night quiet of the inn. She climbed the back stairs to her room, where a small bundle lay neatly folded in front of her door. Sera bent to read the sticky note lying on top.

Sorry.

It was her coat, hat, scarf, and gloves. She picked them up and slipped inside her room. Tomorrow. Tomorrow she would fix this. Kem meant too much to her to let him slip away.

Repairs
(6 days until Christmas)

The next morning, Sera hoped Kem would break away for a bit between the breakfast and lunch rushes. He often had, giving them some time together before he had to report back to the kitchen. But of course, that was the day that chaos took over the inn.

Sera came down the stairs that morning just as Langdon ran up them in his work clothes, heading to fix a leaky pipe. The morning receptionist called in sick, which meant Felicity was manning the desk, until Mrs. Warble came out frantic about an issue with the produce delivery. Felicity grabbed Sera, gave her a thirty-second rundown on the front desk, and left her there.

Sera prayed that the desk would stay quiet until Felicity got back, not at all confident that her thirty-second training was enough to get her through. And so, naturally, the phone rang nonstop, guests calling down room service orders and reporting a broken heater and asking about the weather forecast. After biting back a snarky recommendation about a few good weather apps, Sera reflected that she much preferred being behind her camera to being behind the front desk.

She saw Kem leave the kitchen for his break once the lunch rush was over, but she was tied up with two different guests who had both locked their keys in their rooms. Kem glanced at her, and she could see the misery on his face from across the lobby. While she fumbled through spare keys, he walked out of the inn.

Thankfully, the door had barely swung closed behind him before it opened again for the afternoon shift receptionist. Gladly turning control of the desk over to him, Sera dashed upstairs for her coat and ran out the door after Kem.

He hadn't gone far, walking slowly down the street and kicking at clumps of ice. Sera jogged after him.

"Kem, wait!" she called out. He turned, his eyebrows lifting. Just as she caught up to him, Sera hit an icy patch and slipped. With a yelp, she grabbed him around the neck. He lost his footing, and they both landed in the snow piled off to the side with a soft *whump*. Sera lifted her head and found Kem's hazel eyes inches from her own. The last time they'd been this close… She gulped, fighting to slow her racing heart.

"Do you always tackle men in the street like this?" Kem asked, his teasing smile only half the size it normally was.

Sera grimaced. "Only when I'm hoping to make a good impression."

Kem huffed a brief laugh and looked down. "I didn't make much of a good impression last night," he said quietly. "I'm so sorry, Sera. I promised I wouldn't do anything like that. I just thought you meant—I got carried away."

"I did mean that. I mean, I meant, well, you didn't get carried away. Or maybe we both did together." Sera pinched her lips together before she could babble any more nonsense. Taking a deep breath through her nose, she tried again. "What I'm trying to say is, I didn't run away because you scared me off or anything like that. It's just…"

"Someone hurt you," Kem said. He reached out and touched the skin beneath her left cheekbone. Although his gloves were covered with snow, the gesture sent a sudden rush of warmth through her face.

"How did you know?" Sera asked, her stomach clenching.

Kem shrugged. "The day you came, after you freaked out in the library, you touched your cheek. You did it again last night."

Embarrassed, Sera said, "He was good at putting on a face. I didn't know he was like that. It's not like—"

"Sera." Kem's voice was firm, but kind. "You don't have to explain yourself. Not to me, not to anyone." He stood up, brushing snow off his pants, then reached down to help Sera up. "Are you making a habit of trying to catch hypothermia every time I'm around? You're soaked."

"So are you," Sera said apologetically. "I didn't actually mean to tackle you in order to have this conversation."

"Come on, let's get back to the inn and dry off," Kem said. Hesitantly, he offered his arm. Sera took it, and for the first time that day, she saw a real smile spread on his face.

"I'm sorry I ran off last night," she said as they set off trudging uphill to the inn.

"Thanks for coming to talk to me." Kem gave her a sideways glance. "You looked so miserable at the front desk this morning, I was afraid you'd never speak to me again."

Sera burst out laughing. "That had nothing to do with you. I'm just not cut out for customer service." Drawing together her courage, she asked, "Will you give me another chance?"

"Give *you* another chance?" Kem sounded so shocked that Sera's heart dropped. Then he continued, "That's what I should be asking! You're sure you don't hate me?"

"How could I hate you?"

"Ha. If you're not holding the ammo, I won't hand it to you." He pulled her arm in tighter. "You know, Mrs. Warble will be crowing for weeks."

"Let her crow." Sera leaned her head against Kem's shoulder. "It's worth it."

Langdon couldn't believe the morning he'd had. He'd fixed two leaky pipes, a faulty heater, a closet door, a window stuck open (who had decided to open the blasted window in the dead of winter?!), and a shelf in the library that had collapsed. Dragging himself out of the library, he glanced at his watch and grimaced. It was two o'clock, and he hadn't eaten anything since grabbing a bowl of oatmeal from the kitchen that morning.

He'd remained the primary handyman for the inn as a matter

of pride, but after that string of disasters, he thought maybe it was time to retire from that particular position. Let somebody else climb under sinks for a change.

A door behind him opened, and he heard Felicity call his name. Turning around, he said, "Please don't tell me something else is broken."

Felicity just laughed and jerked her head inside her office. He followed her in, his stomach jumping. He'd been waiting for a free second to talk to her all day, but now that they were here alone, his nerves buzzed. Once he told her, there was no going back.

"They had baked potato soup for lunch," Felicity said, nodding to a bowl on the table. "I saved some for you before it all disappeared."

"You are an angel," Langdon said, pausing only to kiss her briefly before he inhaled the soup. After scraping the last drops from the bowl, he leaned back in his chair and looked at Felicity. Her golden hair curled gently down her back and over her shoulders. She bent over some papers on her desk, reading with her lips moving silently. Then, as if she'd felt his gaze, she looked up. Her eyebrows pulled together, a tiny wrinkle deepening between them.

"What's wrong?"

Langdon blinked. "Wrong?"

"If you clench your teeth any tighter, they're going to shatter."

With some effort, Langdon relaxed his jaw. "Nothing's wrong. I'm just a little tired."

Felicity wasn't buying it. "And?"

He blew out a breath. "And I told Sera last night that you and I would fly home with her for Christmas. That is—if you want to. And if you think it's a good idea. I know the inn is busy at Christmas. Today was proof of that." He ran a hand through his sweaty hair. "Maybe it was a terrible idea. We can't just leave the inn. We have responsibilities here, and—"

"Langdon." Felicity stood slowly, her eyes dancing. "You're really thinking about going home for Christmas?"

Her face shone with delight. One by one, Langdon's misgivings fell away in the face of her enthusiasm. Relenting, he said, "Do you think you could stand spending Christmas with me and my family?"

Felicity flew around the desk and embraced him, sweaty shirt and all. "I think that's the loveliest thing I've ever heard."

"All right." Langdon drew in a shaky breath. "I'll book the tickets. We're going home in four days."

THE NIGHT BEFORE
(3 DAYS UNTIL CHRISTMAS)

The next few days flew by in a haze of preparations. Langdon spent most of the time with a nervous ache in his stomach, which only eased when he saw Felicity and Seraphina chatting and laughing together as if they were already sisters. Whatever grudges his family might hold against him, he felt confident they would be kind to Felicity. And she needed this, as much as he did or more.

Late the night before the flight, Langdon walked into the kitchen to sneak some of the leftover cake from the fridge. But the kitchen wasn't entirely deserted. Sera and Kem sat at a table in the corner, flipping cards over at a furious pace until they both lunged to slap the pile of cards in the middle.

"Cheater!" Sera said, smacking Kem's hand. "I was totally there first!"

"Whatever," Kem laughed, scooping the cards over to his side and straightening them into a pile. "My hand was on the bottom. You can't argue with that."

Langdon walked over and leaned his knuckles on the table. Instantly, Kem stiffened. "Mr. Hyatt," he said awkwardly, glancing at Sera. "Hi."

Sera made a face. "Don't Mr. Hyatt him. That's weird. If we're dating, he's got to be Langdon."

Kem looked uncertainly from Sera to Langdon, who did his best to hold on to his stern expression in spite of his relief that they'd worked things out. Leaning down on his elbows, Langdon said, "Who said anything about dating?"

Sera groaned. "Langdon, don't even. Not unless you want me to tell Felicity about the time you were blasting Spice Girls and—"

"That's not even what happened!" he interrupted, putting a hand in front of her face. "My point, Kemuel Martin Lancaster, is that I have an awful lot of information about you, given that you work for me. And if I get even the slightest hint that my sister is unhappy…"

"You never will," Kem said fervently. "And to be honest, sir, if I did anything Sera didn't appreciate, she'd probably just chop my windpipe anyway. She's given me vivid details about the self-defense class she took."

"Good." Langdon winked at Sera, who rolled her eyes at him.

"Don't you need to go pack or something?" she asked, raising an eyebrow.

"Eh. We're not leaving until the afternoon. I could stay and play a round."

"Go pack."

Langdon chuckled. "Fine. I know when I'm not wanted."

He went to the fridge, took out a piece of cake, and headed for the door. Just before he exited, Sera called, "By the way, I'm going to meet Kem's grandparents tomorrow. He'll drive me to the airport, so I'll meet you guys there."

"You two behave yourselves," Langdon called, leaving the kitchen. He planned to head back to his house and start packing, but he noticed a light still shining from under Felicity's office door. He walked over and knocked softly on the door.

"It's me," he said when she didn't respond to his knock. After a second, he heard the lock turn. He took that as an invitation and pushed the door open.

Felicity sat on the floor in a corner. With her knees pulled up to her chest, she flipped through a massive binder full of pictures. Her family album.

Without speaking, Langdon sat beside her and set the cake next to her. She took a forkful gladly.

"What if they all hate me?" Felicity whispered. Although she was looking at pictures of her family, Langdon knew it was his family that had her worried.

"I wish I knew more that I could tell you about them," he said. "But I know you well enough to know that no one could ever hate you. And however things go with the rest of the family, we have Seraphina."

Felicity smiled. "She's a gem, isn't she? Whoever hired her on must be a genius."

Putting an arm around her, Langdon rested his forehead on the top of her head, breathing in the coconut scent of her hair. "I'm not going to argue with you. I'm glad you did."

"Are you?"

Straightening, he met Felicity's worried gaze. "What do you mean?"

"You aren't upset that I forced you into reconnecting with your family?"

"Oh, Liss." Langdon pulled her tighter into his embrace. "I've been trying to find my way home for twelve years. You've finally given me both the chance and the courage."

FLIGHT
(2 DAYS UNTIL CHRISTMAS)

That night, Sera didn't fall asleep until well after midnight. She woke at two, in a panic that she'd slept in and missed Kem. She woke at three, convinced it was time to get up and finish packing. She woke at four and worried about meeting Kem's grandparents, about getting to the airport in time, about her family's reaction to Langdon walking in the door. About four-thirty, she got sick of worrying and went to take a hot shower.

Once she'd gotten ready and finished packing, she made her way downstairs, where the morning kitchen crew was already moving in a bleary sort of hurry to get breakfast out for the early risers. Sera took a cup of cocoa and walked to the parlor. The world outside the large parlor windows was still dark, lit only by stars and streetlamps. It had started to snow again. Flakes drifted down slowly, lazily, settling onto the cushion of snow already fallen.

"Couldn't sleep?" Felicity asked, coming up behind her.

Sera shook her head. "You either?"

"Not on a day like today. I'm half-expecting the inn to burn down or the airport to explode. Something disastrous that's going to stop us from going."

"I know what you mean." Sera laughed softly. "Just six weeks ago, I thought we'd never have our family together for Christmas again. It seems impossible that it's going to happen today." She reached out and squeezed Felicity's arm. "I'm glad you'll be there. This wouldn't have ever happened without you."

Felicity's eyes brimmed with tears even as she smiled. She gave Sera a tight hug. "I couldn't have ever hoped for a better future sister-in-law." Sniffing, she nodded toward the window. "Looks like we aren't the only ones getting an early start this morning."

Kem trudged up the sidewalk, his face buried in a thick scarf, a dusting of snow on his hat and coat. He glanced up at the window where Sera and Felicity stood, and his eyes—the only visible part of his face—crinkled up.

"I'm glad you two finally figured out you were in love," Felicity said matter-of-factly.

Sera's cheeks burned. "Felicity!"

"What? You guys spent weeks being both adorable and totally clueless."

"At least it didn't take us five years," Sera grumped good-naturedly.

"True. But then, Kem didn't dump a three-tiered cake on your best dress the first time you met."

The front door opened with a swirl of flurries. Kem stamped the snow from his boots and tugged the scarf down from his face. "Are you two the new watchdogs for the inn?"

"You bet," Sera said. "We're here to keep the riffraff out."

"Surely you couldn't think someone with a face like this could be riffraff," Kem said, looking upward with an angelic expression.

"All right, you two, go flirt somewhere else," Felicity said, pushing Sera toward the door. "Some of us have work to do before we go. I'll see you at the airport."

———

Kem's grandmother was every bit as sweet and charming as Sera expected. And it was perfectly obvious where Kem got his penchant for baking from. Not only did she have cinnamon crumble muffins and baked apples ready for them when they got there, she bustled around making toffee while they ate. She and his grandpa took turns asking Sera rapid-fire questions about her interests, her job, and whether Kem was treating her well. More than once, they got Kem squirming with a pointed question or a story about Darling Little Kem, which Sera enjoyed just as much as the baked goods.

When it came time to leave, Sera was sorry to say goodbye to the pair. Nana Wendy (as she'd insisted Sera call her) sent them on their way with a bag of cookies and toffee, but not before demanding (in the most delightful way) that Kem bring her around more often once she returned from Arizona.

The drive to the airport was a quiet one. As thrilled as Sera was about the Christmas to come, she couldn't help wishing that she didn't have to leave Kem behind to be there.

"Are you nervous?" Kem asked, reaching over and taking her hand in his.

"A little." Sera squeezed his hand. "Mostly that my parents will keel over from the shock."

Kem laughed. "I'm happy for you," he said, pulling to the departures curb. "Everything is going to be perfect."

They both climbed out of the car and went to the back for her bags. With her backpack on and her suitcase beside her, Sera reached out and hugged Kem tightly. "Not quite perfect," she murmured, burying her face in the front of his coat. With her heart thudding in her chest, she looked up at him. "I'm sorry I ran away the last time you kissed me."

A slow smile deepened Kem's dimples. "Is that an invitation?"

Sera shrugged, feeling her cheeks grow pink. With the snow falling gently around them, Kem leaned in and kissed her softly.

"Now promise me," he said quietly, pulling her tight and speaking into her ear, "that next time I kiss you, you won't take off and leave me."

Sera laughed. "It's a promise."

"Good." He stepped away, letting go of her with obvious reluctance. "Have the very best Christmas, Seraphina."

Sera floated through check-in and security, half dizzy with delight and anticipation. She made it to the gate and sat down, only to notice a candy-cane-striped package in her backpack that hadn't been there before. Pulling it out, she found a tag in Kem's handwriting.

For when you try to give yourself hypothermia while I'm not around.

Sera unwrapped the package and found a quart-sized bag of hot chocolate mix, labeled *a la Kem* with permanent marker. She tucked it safely into an inside pocket. As much as she loved her family, she was definitely not sharing that.

Time dragged on impossibly slowly. The waiting area gradually filled with white-haired couples, teenagers with headphones on, and families with tiny, adorable kids singing Jingle Bells and oohing over the airplanes. The clock ticked closer and closer to departure time. Sera began checking the terminal nervously for Langdon and Felicity.

Half an hour before departure, the woman at the desk picked up her microphone. "Welcome to Starwind Airlines flight 262," she droned, her words barely comprehensible over the speakers. "At this time we'll be boarding all passengers in need of extra assistance."

Sera's heart kicked into high gear. She sent a quick glance around the terminal, then pulled out her phone and shot a text to Langdon. *Where are you? They're boarding.*

Her knee bounced up and down through the boarding of the Elite Starwind Fliers, followed by boarding group A. When they reached boarding group B—the one listed on her ticket—Sera grabbed her phone again and called Langdon.

"This is Langdon Hyatt. I can't get to my phone right now, so leave your name and number and I'll get back to you."

"You've got to be kidding me," Sera muttered, hanging up and dialing Felicity.

"Felicity here. Or...not here, actually. Leave me a message."

"Where are you?" Sera hissed, hanging up and dialing Langdon again. Straight to voicemail again.

Unbelievable. Had he bailed in the end? Had he ever even really meant to come with her? Felicity had, Sera was sure of it. But she was also Langdon's fiancée. If he had decided not to come, she would have stuck with him.

Tears pricked at Sera's eyes. She forced them back. "They might just be running late," she mumbled to herself, taking a deep breath. "Maybe security is crazy. They'll be here. They have to be here."

Group B boarded, and group C. The woman at the desk looked at Sera questioningly, but Sera couldn't get on that plane yet, not until there was absolutely no chance that her brother was making it. She called both of them again and got their voicemails.

The clock that had been so interminably slow now ticked on absurdly fast. The woman at the desk picked up her microphone again.

"Passengers Seraphina Hyatt, Langdon Hyatt, and Felicity Renner, please report to gate 7 for Starwind flight 626."

The woman looked at Sera expectantly. Sera made one last, futile attempt to call.

It looked like Christmas wasn't going to be so perfect after all.

"Final call for passengers Seraphina Hyatt, Langdon Hyatt, and Felicity Renner."

With the weight of a shattered dream on her shoulders, Sera dragged herself up from her chair. As slowly as she dared, she walked to the desk, looking over her shoulder almost the entire time with the dim hope that she'd see Langdon and Felicity running toward her.

No such luck. Sera reached the ticket scanner and pulled up the ticket on her phone, her heart cracking in a thousand places. The woman lifted her scanner to scan the screen. Impulsively, Sera snatched the phone back.

"Ma'am, I have to scan your ticket," the woman said impatiently.

"I'm not going without him," Sera said, determination flooding her. "Not now."

"Pardon?"

But Sera was long gone, ducking and weaving around Christmas travelers, already on her phone again. This time, someone picked up.

"Kem," Sera said, relieved.

"Aren't you supposed to be on the plane?"

"Langdon and Felicity never showed."

Kem didn't hesitate. "Be there in twenty minutes."

The snow had gotten heavier while she'd been in the airport. Sera pulled her hat down tighter and squinted through the fat flakes at the cars rolling slowly by. Her chest relaxed at the sight of Kem's car pulling over to the curb. She hopped in almost before he'd stopped. The warm air hit her like a welcome hug.

"I'm going to kill him," she growled, slamming the door behind her. "I'm going to kill him for making me late for Christmas Eve, and then I'm going to drag him home by the ear."

Kem's eyebrows pulled together, knitting worriedly. "Have you tried calling them?"

"They're not answering."

They drove in silence through the thick snow, the car's tires kicking up slush as they crawled along the freeway. Traffic was awful. Everybody drove slowly, carefully, windshield wipers flicking snow off. On the far side, a couple of cars were on the side of the road, already under a thick coat of snow.

When they reached Starling, Sera finally found her voice. "What if he's running away again?" she whispered.

The car slipped off to the side a bit as the road tilted uphill, then got traction again. Kem's hands tightened on the steering wheel. "That's not what I'm worried about," he said. His jaw was tight as he guided the car to a parking spot. "Sorry, I don't want to go any farther up in this snow."

His meaning settled in. In spite of the warm air in the car, Sera felt suddenly cold. As soon as he'd parked, Sera pushed her door open and started running up the hill.

"Sera!" Kem called, slipping and catching his balance again as he ran after her. "Sera, wait!"

But she couldn't wait. The icy air seared her lungs, and a painful stitch pierced her side. Still, she ran, dodging tourists and icy patches until Spirited Inn came into view.

Hopping up the porch stairs, Sera opened the door and darted inside. Mrs. Warble stood at the desk, her eyes widening. "Sera! What on earth are you doing here?"

"Where's Langdon?" Sera panted, clutching the stitch in her side as Kem came in behind her.

"Langdon? He and Felicity left over two hours ago! I thought you were meeting at the airport!"

The words hung in the air, innocent and ominous all at once. Sera reached back and gripped Kem's hand. Both Langdon and Felicity's phones had gone to voicemail without ringing.

"Those cars on the side of the road," Sera whispered, the air squeezing out of her lungs.

"We don't know anything yet," Kem said, taking her by the shoulders. "Don't assume the worst. Mrs. Warble, can you make do without me a little longer?"

The normally unflappable head chef had gone pale. She nodded. "Keep us updated," she called as they went back out the door, her voice considerably weaker than normal.

Over Two Hours Ago
(Still 2 Days until Christmas)

Langdon found Felicity at the front desk, scribbling a long list of notes for Mrs. Warble. He slipped an arm around her waist. She didn't even pause, just wrote faster.

"You know," Langdon said, resting his chin on her shoulder, "you've been giving them detailed instructions for the past three days. And if things really get out of hand, you have a cell phone."

"I don't want them calling me on my cell phone," she murmured, finishing her note with a double underline. "I want to be with you and your family."

His family. Langdon's muscles tightened involuntarily. He'd managed to stay busy enough to avoid thinking about it for a few days, but now the full reality of what he was doing crashed over him. He was going back to face the man who'd loomed over him for so long, whose disapproval weighed on him even years after that final phone call.

"Langdon?" Felicity was looking up at him, her forehead furrowed.

He sighed. "Am I doing the right thing? I'm happy with what I've got here. What if I go back home and it's not enough for them?"

"Then you come right back here and keep doing what makes you happy," Felicity said simply. "But if you don't go today, you won't know whether they just might be as proud of you as I am."

Pulling in his breath and blowing it back out, Langdon took her hand and pulled her toward the door. "Okay. Let's do this."

They collected their bags from where they'd been stacked next to the door, then headed out into the thickly falling snow. Langdon got the bags into the back of his car and went around to the driver's side.

"Hang on!" Felicity exclaimed, spinning around back toward the inn. "I forgot my charger!"

She ran back inside. Langdon turned the key in the ignition, cranking up the heater and shivering in the cold while he waited.

Only a minute or two later, Felicity came out of the inn. She ran down the porch stairs and down the path to where the car was parked. Three feet from the car, her arms flew up in the air, her legs slipped around to an awkward angle, and she went down hard on the icy cement.

Leaping out of the car, Langdon ran around it to see what had happened. She pulled herself up to sit, insisting, "I'm fine, I'm fine, let's get going." But when she went to stand, she grimaced and fell back, one hand on her ankle.

"Let me see," Langdon said. He rolled up the cuff of her jeans and touched the already-swelling ankle.

"It's fine," Felicity said fiercely. "I just rolled it a little. Help me into the car."

"It's turning purple," he protested.

She scowled. "We are not missing our flight just because I twisted my ankle. It'll be fine."

This was a foreboding beginning to their trip. Lifting Felicity to her feet, Langdon helped her to the car, then leaned down to speak to her. "I'm getting an ice pack from the inn. I'll be back."

He searched out the first aid station, grabbed an instant ice pack, and made it back out the door with Mrs. Warble flapping her arms at him to get on his way. He picked his way carefully down the slushy sidewalk, handed the ice pack to Felicity, and finally climbed inside the now-warm car. Leaning back in his seat, he took a fortifying breath.

"You tell me if that ankle gets worse," he said, fixing her with a serious stare. "We can always book another flight if you need to go to the doctor and get it checked out."

"Stop waffling and drive," Felicity said, waving away his concern. "I'll ice it. It'll be okay. We're going to be late if we don't get going."

Langdon pulled out onto the street, flicking his windshield wipers on. He'd cleared off the car before going inside for Felicity, but with the snow coming down the way it was, it was already starting to build up again.

Starling had a dedicated crew that kept the steep slope of

Main Street cleared in the winter. And of course, Langdon and Felicity ended up directly behind the snowplow. A blessing, on the one hand. It meant the street was plenty clear as they made their way downhill. But it also meant that it took them three times as long to get out of town. Langdon caught Felicity checking her watch nervously as they crept closer and closer to the bottom of the slope.

Finally, the snowplow pulled out of the way, and Langdon sped past it. Beside him, Felicity flinched.

"Not too fast," she said, gripping the bar above her window. "The roads are awful out here."

"I'm being careful," he promised, glancing at her pale face. She hated driving in the snow. After an icy road had taken her family, she'd avoided snowy roads at any cost. The fact that she was willing to make this trip in the middle of a bad winter spoke loads about her determination to see it through.

When they reached the highway, they could barely move any faster than they had on the smaller roads. There were two lanes going each way, and both lanes were thick with cars rolling slowly and cautiously through the snow.

"We're going to make it," Langdon said when he caught Felicity checking her watch again, reassuring himself as much as her. "We left in plenty of time. And they'll hurry us through security if our flight is boarding. We're going to be okay."

"Should I call Sera and tell her we're on our way?" Felicity asked.

"She's probably going through all the check-in and security right now. We'll see her soon enough. Don't worry about it."

"Easily said," Felicity grumbled, glancing at her watch yet again.

On and on they crept, the clock ticking incessantly closer to boarding time. At last, the first sign for the airport came into view. Relief poured through Langdon's veins. "See!" he said cheerfully. "We're almost there!"

In response, Felicity reached over and grabbed his knee, her fingers digging into his flesh. Not a good sign. Langdon followed her gaze and saw a car coming the opposite way start to fishtail, sliding back and forth in its lane.

"It's okay," he said automatically, his heart skipping into high gear. "We're in the far lane. He'll get control. We're going to be okay, Liss. We're almost there."

The car drew closer to them, sliding more wildly. Langdon pushed as close to the car in front of them as he dared, desperate to get past the fishtailing car. Felicity's fingers dug into his leg. They were almost there. They were going to get past. They were going to be fine.

With unbelievable precision, the car in the opposite lane lost control completely just as they passed. It slipped neatly through a gap in the cars in the closer lane. Langdon could see the kids in the back seat of the car, eyes and mouths both wide and round, clear and much too close. Then the back end of the car collided with his door in a bone-shattering crunch that didn't drown out Felicity's scream.

After three quick calls, Sera confirmed that Langdon and

Felicity had been checked into the hospital halfway between the inn and the airport. Unfortunately, the woman on the phone couldn't give her any more information. There was nothing else to do but get to the hospital and wait it out.

The hospital was twenty minutes away on a good day. Between the weather and traffic, it took them forty agonizing minutes to reach it. The entire time, Sera wished she could hang onto Kem's hand and squeeze it bloodless; but Kem had both hands on the steering wheel, white-knuckled, his lips pressed into a tight line. She settled for gripping the edge of her seat and staring out the window for any sign of Langdon's car, any hint of how big of a disaster awaited her.

The hospital came into view. Adrenaline rocketed through Sera's veins, driven hard by fear. She took a deep, shaky breath. "I just found my brother," she whispered. "I don't want to lose him again."

"Let's go in and figure out the situation," Kem said, pulling into the parking lot. "Whatever happens, we'll get through it, okay?"

"Okay." With one last fortifying breath, Sera opened the door and stepped out into the snow.

She'd expected a lot of questions and delay once they got inside. But the second she walked into the emergency room waiting area, she spotted Felicity sitting near the window. Her ankle and wrist were both wrapped, and thin, fresh cuts could be seen on her face and arms, along with a deep purple bruise on the side of her forehead.

Felicity looked up and gasped as Sera rushed over to her. The two embraced. Sera could feel Felicity trembling as the words poured out of her.

"Sera, I'm so sorry, I'm so sorry, we were running late but we were almost there and a car slid on the ice, both our phones were smashed, I couldn't remember your number, I just got out and I don't know—" Felicity choked and buried her face in Sera's shoulder. Sera held her, fighting to process what was going on.

"You're okay, though?" she asked, her voice squeaky and uneven.

"Yes. Just some cuts and bruises. The stupid ankle isn't even from the crash, just me being a klutz. The people in the other car were fine, too, mostly just shaken. But the back end of the car slid right into Langdon's door." Felicity tightened her grip on Sera's coat. "I'm going to lose him, too. I'm going to lose him the way I lost everyone else. His head…there was blood everywhere. He was barely breathing."

Kem joined them, kneeling next to Felicity and putting a hand on her knee. "I just talked to a nurse," he said, his voice deeper than normal. "Langdon is going to be fine. They've got him stabilized, and they're patching him up now. His shoulder is going to need surgery, so they're working to make that happen. The nurse said the doctor will be out with more information in a while, but the important thing is that he'll be okay."

Felicity raised her head, her eyes red and weary. "He's not going to die?"

"No, Felicity," Kem said gently. His gaze moved to Sera, who felt her own eyes tearing up. "Everything's going to be okay."

Felicity hugged Sera one more time, tight enough to squeeze the air out. Then she slumped back in her chair, resting her head against the wall and closing her eyes. Kem squeezed Sera's shoulder and whispered that he was going to call the inn. Sera sat in the chair beside Felicity, striving to slow her heartbeat back to a normal pace.

"It's been horrible," Felicity whispered, her eyes still closed. "I just keep playing the moment over and over in my mind, and it mixes up with every horrible scene I've imagined for the crash that killed my family. And I was so worried you'd just give up and fly home without us, that you'd hate us and never come back. And if Langdon…I would be all alone again."

A lump swelled in Sera's throat. "Never," she said firmly, taking Felicity's uninjured hand and squeezing it gently. "You don't have to be alone anymore. You have a second family now, and I'm not going anywhere."

They waited for another forty minutes before a doctor finally came out to speak to them. Felicity leaped to her feet, limping across the room so fast that Sera and Kem had to hurry to keep up with her. "How is he?" Felicity asked breathlessly.

"He's going to recover with time," the doctor said, practiced calm ringing in his voice. "He's got broken ribs, a fractured leg, and a broken shoulder, but all of those things will heal. We have him scheduled for surgery for his shoulder in a couple of hours. You're welcome to go in and see him. He's been in and out of consciousness, but he's heavily medicated and may not be very responsive. Still, it would be good for him to see that he has some support."

Felicity was already pushing past the doctor to get back there. Sera and Kem walked on either side of her to support her as they passed through the door, into the overwhelming smell of antiseptic and the persistent sound of beeping. The doctor pointed them into a room, and Sera and Felicity went in, Kem staying out in the hall to give them a moment.

Langdon lay on the bed with his eyes closed, his chest moving with shallow breaths. The left side of his face was swollen and mottled with bruises and cuts. A cast covered one leg, and a sling held his arm in place. Felicity stood beside him, perfectly still, her eyes riveted on the rise and fall of his chest. Sera stood just behind her and saw the moment his eyes fluttered open and fixed on Felicity's face.

"Liss," he murmured, his voice thick. "You're okay."

"I'm fine," she said, touching his unbandaged arm lightly.

"I'm sorry. The car…"

"It's not your fault. Nobody could have avoided that. We're both alive and that's what matters."

Sera felt inexplicably like shrinking away and hiding when Langdon's eyes slid over to her. She smiled, trying for some show of strength, but Langdon's eyebrows drew together in a moment of painful realization. "I ruined everything, didn't I?" he mumbled, closing his eyes.

Heart twisting, Sera stepped closer. "No! You can't—this wasn't your fault, Lang."

"But I'm missing Christmas again." The words were so faint she could barely hear them. Langdon's head nestled deeper into the pillow in sleep.

Sera stared down at him for a long moment, her mind racing. "I'll be right back," she said to Felicity, and ducked out into the hallway.

Kem, waiting just outside the door, looked at her questioningly. "Everything okay?"

"It's going to be," Sera said fiercely. "I've got to make a phone call."

CHRISTMAS DAY

The doctors kept Langdon in the hospital through Christmas Eve. With all the pain meds he was on, Langdon was only vaguely aware of Sera and Kem being there in the morning. By the time his head cleared a little more in the afternoon, only Felicity was there. He did his best to conceal the pang of disappointment that came with knowing Sera had left without him. He vividly remembered how she'd fought against staying through Christmas, and he understood why she'd gone. She had to make up for his mistakes. But it didn't make it any easier to know that he'd missed his chance yet again.

Thankfully, he had Felicity. Sweet, solid Felicity. Langdon could see the toll that the accident had taken on her, but she was cheerful and helpful, up and around pouring him water and adjusting his blankets and doing more than she probably should have, even when Langdon insisted she should be resting.

After dinner, she turned on a movie and promptly fell asleep with her head on the bed next to him. Langdon lost any interest in watching the movie, busy instead watching the woman who had believed in him and bolstered him in a way he'd never known before. He moved his uninjured hand closer to her, stroking his fingers through her soft, golden hair.

For so many years, he'd watched Christmases go by like one missed chance after another. But with Felicity at his side, this disaster felt more like a setback instead of another failure. Her quiet confidence assured him that, somehow or other, everything would come out all right in the end.

With his hand resting on Felicity's head and peace resting in his heart, Langdon leaned back into his pillows and slept.

Christmas morning, Langdon woke up to the sound of whispering. He opened his eyes, disoriented for a moment by the stark white walls before remembering where he was. Felicity stood whispering with Kem next to the door. Langdon struggled to sit up, a groan escaping him as his ribs and shoulder spiked with pain.

Felicity stepped to his side, laying a hand on his shoulder. "Relax, sweetheart. If you get all worked up, the doctor might change her mind about releasing you this morning."

"What are you doing here?" Langdon asked Kem groggily. "You should be at home. It's Christmas."

Kem grinned. "I know. That's why I'm here."

"Kem's helping me get you home," Felicity said quickly. She gave Kem a look that was a little stern for the occasion, Langdon thought vaguely, especially if the guy had given up his Christmas morning to spend at the hospital.

"Are they really going to let me out?" The thought of not having to eat hospital food for Christmas dinner was definitely a good one.

"The doctor's on her way to give you a final check," Felicity said. "Once she's satisfied and signs off on the paperwork, we'll load up into the car and head home."

On her way turned out to be a relative term. It was another three hours before he was finally discharged, and even then, a blunt nurse insisted on pushing him in a wheelchair to the front door, in spite of Kem's insistence that he could do it. At the car, the nurse watched with narrow eyes and tight lips as they helped Langdon into his seat. She spent another ten minutes explaining how to properly fold and unfold the wheelchair, then watched Kem and Felicity do it until she was satisfied that they wouldn't break it.

At last, they were on their way. The snow had stopped, the sun was out, and the roads were clear. Even so, Langdon couldn't stop watching the cars in the opposite lane, waiting for one of them to spin out. After ten minutes, he had to close his eyes to keep himself from expecting a collision every time a car passed.

He didn't open his eyes again until the car had stopped. With the sun reflecting off the bright snow, he had to blink and squint for a few seconds before he realized where they were. "The inn?"

he said, his heart sinking a little. "Aren't we going home?"

"We can go home right after this," Felicity said, already out of the car and opening his door. "I know you must be exhausted, but just hang in there for a few minutes."

Kem got the wheelchair open, and he and Felicity helped Langdon into it. As Felicity pushed the wheelchair toward the ramp leading up to the porch, the front door of the inn flew open. Sera came out, practically skipping down the walk to join them.

"Sera!" Langdon couldn't tell if he was incensed or overjoyed. "What are you doing here? You're supposed to be at home!"

"You think I was going home without you?" Sera scoffed, passing a wink over his head at Felicity.

"Yes! It's Christmas! I'm not going to be able to travel for ages, Phina. You have to go home. What about everything you said about Mom and stockings?"

"Calm down, Lang." Sera didn't sound nearly worked up enough about it. "Things have a way of working out."

"Save your energy," Felicity said, resting a hand on his unhurt shoulder. "Let's get you inside, and then we can talk about Christmas."

Sera and Kem both laughed. Slowly, the strange lightheartedness of the laughter filtered past the pain medication. Langdon glanced sideways at Sera, who was incontrovertibly *beaming*. There was no other word for it. Something was going on. But before his muddled reasoning could make it any further, they'd reached the front door. Sera opened it, and Felicity wheeled him inside.

A giant banner hung from the second-story railing, declaring *Welcome Home* for all to see. Staff members poked their heads out from various rooms with cries of "Merry Christmas!" and "Glad you're back!" But Felicity had picked up speed, and she didn't stop until they'd reached the elevator, held open by Mr. Johansen. Up to the third floor they went, around the corner to the largest of the private dining rooms. A sign hung on the door, elegantly declaring the room *Reserved*.

Felicity, Kem, and Sera all exchanged a glance, then Sera looked down at him. Langdon saw how her smile had suddenly grown nervous, and he felt his own heartbeat kick up a little higher. "Okay," Sera said. She flexed her fingers, then reached for the door.

The room was large enough for thirty people to spread out comfortably. But at the moment, everyone in the room had clustered inside the doorway, most of them holding onto each other in a tight, anxious sort of way. Langdon scanned their faces, and his breath caught in his sore chest.

They were all there. Rhett, still tall but no longer gangly, looking sharp and professional in a button-down shirt and square-framed glasses. Elliott, looking more relaxed in jeans and a t-shirt, with a woman at his side and a toddler peering out from behind his legs. His mom, just the same but with a few extra gray hairs.

And his dad.

They stood for a long moment, two lines of people staring each other down uncertainly, two rows of strangers who shouldn't have been strangers. And then his mother broke the invisible barrier between them, taking two half-running-steps forward and dropping to her knees, hugging her injured son gently. Langdon returned the embrace, his good arm wrapped around her back, his eyes squeezed shut against the wall of tears that flooded him.

"I brought your stocking," she choked out into his shoulder. The entire room broke into laughter, including his mom. She pulled back, wiping her eyes and chuckling at herself. "Twelve years of imagining what I wanted to say to you, and that's what I lead with."

"Thanks, Mom," Langdon said, the words fitting neatly into his mouth and filling the hole that had sat empty in his heart for so many years. He looked up, searching out his father and finding the man with silent tears streaming down his face. That was all it took to break down the last of Langdon's composure. His dad stepped forward and stretched out a hand. Langdon gripped it tightly.

"I'm sorry, Dad," he said, the words tumbling out of him. No matter how many times he'd written the words, it wasn't enough, and now they all broke free in a wild rush. "I'm sorry for everything I said. I'm sorry for all the times I couldn't do enough. I'm—"

"Son." His dad held up a hand, obviously fighting to keep his voice steady enough to speak. "Don't—I'm the one who owes all the apologies. I didn't realize until it was too late how much of an idiot I'd been. When you said—said that you'd let me down—Langdon, I can't tell you how many times I've wished..." His dad swallowed, opened his mouth, swallowed again and shook his head. Langdon sat in silent shock, wondering if this was all

113

going to turn out to be some morphine-induced dream. Finally, his dad recovered enough to say, "The inn is incredible, son. I'm so proud of you."

Langdon squeezed his father's hand, unable to find words big enough to explain what that simple statement had done to his heart.

Of course, Rhett was there to break down the tear-fest. "Sera keeps raving about the food in this place," he announced. "I want to know if she's telling the truth, or if she's biased because of that kid over there with the dimples."

"Rhett," Sera groaned, reddening, but Kem just laughed.

"I'll let Mrs. Warble know to send up lunch," he said.

"Thanks, Kem," Sera said, squeezing his hand to let him know that she wasn't just talking about lunch. He smiled, the warmth in his eyes melting her soul into a puddle, then stepped through the door.

Felicity bent down to whisper into Langdon's ear, worry crinkling her brow. "Should I take you home? We didn't want this to be too much for you. You can go home and rest. Everyone would understand."

"Are you kidding?" Langdon said. "This is home right here. Them and you. There is nowhere else I'd rather be."

Rhett declared lunch every bit as high quality as Sera had boasted, and heartily approved of the pie, cake, and trifle that Kem had sent up as well. They stayed in there, eating and talking and reconnecting, for hours. Langdon had been positioned in the armchair with enough pillows to fill three beds, and he warded off any hint that he should be resting. At least, until he nodded off mid-sentence as he talked through the specifics of a kitchen renovation with his dad. When he woke again, Felicity and his mom joined forces to insist that he go lie down.

Sera followed Langdon and Felicity out of the room, her stomach twisting a little. Once they were away from the rest of the family, she bent down and asked quietly, "Do you mind that I told them?"

"Mind?" Langdon shook his head, slowly and carefully. "No, Sera. I don't mind at all." He tilted his head, listening to quiet strains of violin music that floated through the air.

Sera cocked an ear as well. "I have to know," she said, her expression a little sheepish, "who plays the violin?"

Langdon's eyes popped. "You can hear it?"

"Just barely. It's beautiful. I've heard it now and again, but I always assumed it was a recording." Judging by the way her eyebrows drew together, she didn't assume that anymore. "Who is it?"

For a second, Langdon thought about telling the whole story. But it was a big story, and he was exhausted. He exchanged glances with Felicity—the only person he'd ever told about the violinist—and settled for a smaller tale. "It's a guest. The girl who convinced me to buy the inn and fix it up. She told me my family would be proud of what I did here." He grinned. "I think it's her way of saying *I told you so.*"

"All right, enough stalling," Felicity said, pushing the

wheelchair forward. "You can revel in your family's praise after you've had a nap."

"Thank you, Phina," Langdon called back softly. As Felicity pushed him into the elevator, he caught sight of a little girl at the end of the hall in a vintage-looking blue dress, a violin tucked under her chin. She beamed, finished her song with a flourish, and vanished.

Want to know how Spirited Inn got started?
Read the short story at
bajgoodson.com/blog/short-story-contest-
winner-indigo-wood-september-2019

Acknowledgments

Many thanks to my initial readers, Becca, Sophia, and Kammi, whose enthusiasm overcame my doubts; to Baj, whose writing prompt gave Spirited Inn its soul; and to all the friends who ask how my writing's going. I'd never have the courage to send my words into the world without you wonderful people.

My forever thanks to my parents and siblings. I couldn't ask for a better bunch of human beings to have in my corner. Thanks for your listening ears.

And of course, the deepest thanks of my heart go to my husband, with his unfailing reassurances that my manuscripts are not a giant trash fire, and to my girls, who inspire me daily with their creativity and joy. I love you to outer space and back.

ABOUT THE AUTHOR

Indigo lives with her husband and two daughters in a small brick house surrounded by a scurry of squirrels and a coil of garter snakes. When she's not writing or reading, she's crocheting, baking, or adventuring with her family. Adventures involving nature and ending with ice cream are highly preferred, though a dragon will never be turned down. You can find her gushing about her favorite books on Instagram (@indi.go.wood).

Made in the USA
Monee, IL
26 November 2019